PARIS LOVE MATCH

NIGEL BLACKWELL

ALVESCOT PUBLISHING

Paris *Love* **Match**

ISBN: 978-1-942536-06-2

For my wife and daughter,
my favorite world travelers.
It's a big, wide world.
And so much better with you in it.
Love you.

Sometimes not getting what you want is a remarkable stroke of luck.

— DALAI LAMA

CHAPTER ONE

Boucher Brunwald stepped onto the balcony of his penthouse suite. The October air chilled the dictator's lungs and washed the last of a good night's sleep from his face. He buttoned his coat and stared down the Champs-Élysées. It was six-thirty in the morning and already Maître d's were fussing over white tablecloths and packing patrons knee-to-knee in tiny cafés. Shops were coming to life. Between rows of bare trees, crepe stands did a brisk trade. It was business as usual in Paris.

The day was dawning in his country too. The country to which, even though he technically still ruled, he would never return. He'd enjoyed the luxurious lifestyle of a dictator and the power of ruling with an iron fist, but the country was broke and its citizens ready to revolt.

The door behind him opened, and his bodyguard stepped onto the balcony. He was a giant of a man dressed in a black suit that barely concealed his holstered Glock. The man cracked his knuckles. "You shouldn't be out here."

Brunwald grunted. Kuznik never relaxed. Even now, he could see the man's eyes scanning the building opposite, looking for faces at windows or chinks in the glass that might conceal a rifle.

But Kuznik wasn't the boss and they were hours from success. Brunwald cleared his throat. "I needed the air."

Kuznik kept his eyes scanning. "It's always dangerous in a city."

Brunwald gave a short laugh. "Paris is not a city."

The man sneered, his eyes examining a dark patch in a window to their right.

Brunwald brought his fingers to a point. "It's an idea, a dream, a hope."

Kuznik surveyed the street below. "If you say so."

"There is no doubt about it. The French don't love Paris." Brunwald spread his arms. "They love the idea of Paris. They love the idea of the architecture, of the people, of the glamour, the fame. That's what makes this place special. That's what makes the people here special."

"The fame?"

"No! The love of an idea."

"If you say so."

Brunwald laughed then raised his eyebrows. "Which is why it is better to sell the painting here."

"We should have sold it yesterday. In Copenhagen."

Brunwald shook his head. "They offered twice as much here. And it's a simple business transaction. We meet the mob, trade the painting for diamonds, and we're on our way to South America to live out the rest of our days on a beach surrounded by luxury. What could go wrong?"

"If we had sold it yesterday with the other national treasures, we would already be in South America. Now we have to deal with another set of idiots. And when you're dealing with idiots, lots of things can go wrong."

Brunwald waved his hand. "You worry too much. You have more men and more firepower, and, as you say, they're idiots."

"Even idiots can get lucky."

Brunwald stared straight at Kuznik, and dropped his voice an octave. "Then don't give them the chance." He straightened his back. "You've briefed the men?"

"To the letter."

"I won't tolerate failure. Warn them."

"They know, sir."

Brunwald looked back out at the view down the Champs-Élysées. "That man, the one who failed us in Copenhagen ..."

"With the speeding ticket?"

Brunwald grunted his agreement. "It was an unnecessary risk to the operation. Details like that leave tracks. We don't want tracks."

"I took care of it. I sent him home."

Brunwald whipped around. "Home! How?"

"Second class, sir."

Brunwald glowered.

Kuznik smiled. "Face down in a box."

Brunwald's glower melted and he gave a single slow nod. "And the men?"

Kuznik shrugged. "Believe I sent him home."

Brunwald took a deep breath. "Excellent. One more day and we will be done. Then you and I can leave this miserable cold continent once and for all."

"And the men?"

"They will have to go home, too." Brunwald turned and stared Kuznik in the eye. "Second class."

CHAPTER TWO

Piers Chapman gazed across the river to Notre Dame cathedral and cursed to himself. In his rush to catch his train, he'd left his Nikon in the kitchen of his London apartment. On the opposite bank, the morning light mixed with a faint mist and wrapped the centuries-old Gothic masterpiece in a heartbreakingly beautiful bleakness. The French and the tourists, on the other hand, wrapped the place in trash and graffiti. Nothing, he grinned, that Photoshop couldn't fix.

His phone buzzed. Despite having the latest in mobiles, he couldn't bear its stupid musical ring tones. He'd hacked into it the night he had bought it and replaced the lot.

A French number glowed on the display. He pressed *talk*. "Bonjour."

"Monsieur Chapman?"

"Oui."

"You are ready to update the software in our cranes, yes?"

"That's what I'm here for."

"Bon. Shall we say tomorrow at ten?"

"I'm supposed to do it today."

"Non. This is not possible. I have a schedule."

Piers looked up at the vista of Notre Dame. "So do I. I have a ticket home tonight. I didn't even bring a toothbrush."

"Monsieur, if Waterloo Large Construction had brought the correct equipment, no software update would be required."

Piers sighed. "I can't change my plans, and the update will only take a minute."

"Then I shall have to talk to your superiors. I will see you tomorrow. Good day, monsieur." There was a click and the line went dead.

He sighed. Waterloo Large didn't like upsetting the people who paid for their services. He made a bet with himself that the project office would call within two minutes. But two minutes was two minutes, so he crossed the river and joined the line for Notre Dame tours.

On the far bank, he could see the pair of cranes he was to update were stationary. As he debated sneaking into the site and updating them without permission, his phone rang. It wasn't the office number he expected but, then again, it was the number he always expected. He took a deep breath and pressed *talk*. "Hi, mum."

"Piers, you didn't answer."

"Didn't answer when?"

"Three hours ago, when I called."

"I must have been in the Chunnel. Out of range."

"Well you need to keep in touch, dear. You know how your father worries about you when you travel."

Piers gave a wry smile. "If he's that worried, get him to send a text next time."

"Oh, no, dear. Your father and I aren't teenagers."

"Mum, it's just a way to communicate."

"I don't want to communicate. I want to talk."

"Right. Look, I've got to go. Work and all that."

"Of course. But you will keep in touch, won't you? You're not staying long, are you? Over there, I mean. Course you aren't. I'm sure you don't like it over there any more than your father did when he had to go there. 1986. He didn't like it one bit. All olive oil and raw meat. Really, it's no way to enjoy yourself, is it now?"

"Mum, I have to go."

"Yes, you said. Work. Well, hurry home. And stay in well-lit areas with lots of people around. You always hear such terrible stories of people who travel to these foreign places."

"It's France. It's closer than Scotland."

"And that's supposed to recommend the place?"

Piers sighed. "I've got to go. Bye, mum."

Piers held the phone away from his ear until his mother's goodbyes trailed off. When he ended the call, he saw an envelope icon glowing on the display. He opened it.

French want software update delayed to Saturday. Travel office rescheduling tickets. Hotel Lafayette booked under company name. Get a taxi. You know the Per Diem, but don't spend it all. I'll tell the guys Xbox is off tonight.

Piers sighed. Changing his plans was a bummer, but an extra day in Paris would be good.

He stepped out of line. He needed to check into his hotel before taking in the sights. Stuffing his phone in his pocket, he crossed the square outside Notre Dame, and waved at a passing taxi.

CHAPTER THREE

For the first time in weeks, Sidney Roux felt hopeful as she threaded her way through the early morning crowd and crossed the Seine. Her stomach growled at the scent of freshly baked bread drifting from a corner café. She wanted to stop but she didn't dare be late. She had an interview. Her muscles tingled with adrenaline at the thought. She'd finally done it, landed an interview at a fashion house.

She tucked her portfolio under her arm. She had no shortage of designs to show off. Paris had proved to be a fire hose of inspiration. She had searched every alleyway for handmade clothes in hole-in-the-wall shops. She'd studied the vintage pieces she'd discovered at flea markets. She toured department stores so often she could name every single designer they stocked. It had done wonders for her creativity, and now was her chance to prove it.

The polished black and white facade of the fashion house loomed. She adjusted her jacket and smoothed the wrinkles out of a skirt of her own design. Taking a deep breath, she opened the door to her future.

An impossibly slim girl behind a polished marble counter raised her eyebrows expectantly.

"Sidney Roux. I have an interview. Monsieur Charbonneau, the Creative Director."

The girl consulted a calendar. "Roux. Right. I'll page him."

Sidney took a seat in a giant armchair, her adrenaline keeping her bolt upright and smiling. It was so hard to take everything in. It was only five weeks since she'd run away from her crumbling country, but it seemed like forever. She missed her friends and family, of course, but not the secret police. She didn't miss her miserable rat of a boyfriend—who'd turned out to be very married—either.

The receptionist led her to a conference room and the Creative Director arrived. Sidney had to force herself not to wrinkle her nose at the man's exuberantly applied cologne. After a moment's small talk, he asked for her portfolio. Her heart thumped in her throat as she handed it over.

He flipped through the pages, and tapped a drawing with his fingers. "This tightly-structured suit jacket is very cutting edge." He flipped another page, smiling. "And these fabrics. Very eclectic mix. Very nice."

She dared to relax a fraction and images of Fashion Week tumbled into her mind. She saw herself on the runway, being named the next big thing by Vogue, and her collections gracing the covers of magazines all over the world. Her skin tingled with excitement.

The man flipped another page. Her boudoir collection. Lingerie in pastels edged with black and primary colors. The designs would flatter any woman's body type, and she had spent every penny she could afford on the finest silks. They were gorgeous to look at, and made her feel like a goddess when they slid across her skin. When a photographer friend had offered to photograph her in them, she had jumped at the chance.

The man stopped flipping and started studying. She held her breath. Surely he would like them?

He looked up at her and back to the pictures. Was something wrong? His eyes slid back to her and wandered down her suit.

Her skin prickled and she flushed hot. She knew in an instant, modeling them herself had been a mistake.

The man closed the portfolio. "Delightful. Exquisite. In fact, just what I was looking for."

Sidney nodded, her heart pounding so hard she didn't dare speak.

The man smiled. "I think you may have a great career ahead of you, mademoiselle, if you are prepared to work for it. But we should discuss this in a more … agreeable setting. If you are available? This evening?"

Sidney swallowed. "Can't we discuss it now?"

He gave a broad, benign smile, and placed one hand delicately on her knee. "I was thinking over a glass of Bordeaux. In private. At my apartment. Say seven-thirty?" He squeezed her knee. "These fabrics look sensational. I would love to feel them. On you."

She moved her knee away from his hand. "I can't. I could bring samples tomorrow and—"

"You do want launch your career, don't you?" He leaned forward and placed both hands on her knees. "I can do that."

She stood up and he followed, slipping his arms around her waist. She rammed her knee into his groin, and he folded over. He was still groaning on the floor as she slammed the door and stormed out of the building.

She stepped out into the early morning air, wrapped her jacket around herself, and ground her teeth. The bastard. What was it with men that made them think they had the right to drag her to their beds? Smarmy, blackmailing jerk. So much for her big chance. Her only chance. She blew out a long breath and walked toward the Seine, letting the morning air take the edge from the emotions fizzing in her blood.

Raindrops splashed on the sidewalk as she rounded a corner and faced Notre Dame cathedral. The square in front was the usual heaving mass of tourists and trinket sellers. She spotted a taxi cruising for passengers. She had nine euros left in her pocket, maybe enough for a ride, and to keep her outfit dry. She elbowed her way through the crowd, waving at the driver.

On the opposite side of the road she noticed a tall, angular guy with tightly cropped, dark hair. His clothes had the square, shapeless fit that only discount chains could achieve and, without looking, she already knew the hem of his jeans would be a half-inch too short.

He waved to the taxi.

"No!" she shouted. She wasn't going to let another man ruin her day.

She dived for the taxi.

CHAPTER FOUR

Piers slammed the taxi door and sank into a seat that had long since given up any effort to support its occupants. "Hotel Lafayette, si vous—"

The opposite rear door whipped open. Piers' mouth froze half-open with his tongue poking out. His forehead wrinkled and his eyebrows inched closer together. The face of an angel stared at him and he glimpsed the mesmerizing curve of a tight-fitting skirt and long legs bounding into the taxi. The angel leaned back in the seat, and undid the top button of a business suit. His thoughts danced uncomfortably between modesty and the sight of her cleavage.

She ran a hand through long, jet-black hair, flipped one side over her ear, and turned to look at him with deep mocha eyes. She smiled. Big and broad. Intense and confident. A full thousand watts. Her high cheekbones and soft lips underlined her angelic presence. Tiny dimples rippled as she opened her mouth to speak.

Piers held his breath as the sight of her paralyzed his voice.

"Get out," she said.

Piers blinked in shock. "What?"

"Get out."

"What?" The wattage had gone from her smile, but Piers still feared his heart might stop as he looked at her. "But I—"

She leaned across him and yanked at the door handle on his side. "Go on, get out."

The sounds of Paris wafted in through the open door, a hundred languages, all spoken at once.

"I beg your pardon, but I was here first."

"And?"

"Doesn't that mean it's my taxi?"

The voices outside turned to shouts.

She shook her head.

Piers sighed. "I hate to be rude, but I was seated before you arrived, and I was giving the driver the address when you got in."

She huffed. "In Paris there is a certain etiquette regarding taxis."

He raised his eyebrows. "Etiquette?"

She gave a patronizing smile. "I started for the taxi before you. That means it's my taxi."

The driver leaned back over his seat. "Will one of you tell me where we're going?"

Her eyes remained locked on Piers. "I saw it first and I need to keep this outfit dry."

"I was hoping to stay dry, too."

"I need this taxi."

"We could share."

The girl grunted.

"Please," the driver said. "One of you tell me where we're going,"

Piers glanced at the driver. "Hotel La—"

She waved her hand in front of his face. "Non, non. Rue de—"

There was more shouting outside the cab. A large, wet man dived headlong through the open door and across the rear seat. He rolled around, his elbows and knees digging into Piers. The girl lurched away.

Piers opened his mouth, but his throat closed up at the sight of a gun in the man's hand. His heart thumped hard against his ribs. His arms locked solid and his legs felt like lead. He tried to swallow, but his mouth was dry.

The man waved the gun at the driver. "Vite, vite! Drive! Go!"

The driver turned around slowly, his eyes wide and magnetically attracted to the gun.

Piers glimpsed the girl moving her hand toward the door handle. She hadn't reached it before he heard strange popping sounds behind them and the car's rear window exploded in a storm of tiny daggers.

She screamed and rolled forward into the footwell.

The man fired two shots through the hole where the rear window had been. "Go!"

Piers slapped his hands over his ears. He'd never heard a real gun fired. His head rang and his ears hurt. He thought the girl was screaming, but he couldn't be sure. It seemed like every tin drum in the world was making a noise in his ear at once.

The car fishtailed away from the curb and the man lurched to one side, dropping his phone. The driver huddled down, only the top of his head visible above the dashboard.

The man struggled over Piers and grabbed for his phone as it slid around on the floor. He missed it, turned, and fired another shot through the rear window.

The driver took a right-hand corner fast. Piers slid across the seat, crushing up against the man and the girl. The man shouted something unintelligible. Piers pulled himself back onto his side of the car while the man fired more shots. The girl remained in the footwell, her hands clamped over her ears and the man's phone wedged under her knee.

Piers caught a glimpse of a car behind them struggling to take the same corner. It bounced on the curb, smashed into a wall, and disappeared in a cloud of steam. Behind it, he could see a police car come to a halt and two officers getting out.

Finally, the police to the rescue.

He breathed a sigh of relief until he looked down and saw spots of blood on his shirt. He ran his hands over himself. Nothing seemed to hurt. Then he saw the man laid back on the seat, blood pumping from a hole in his shirt.

"Slow down!" Piers yelled at the driver.

The driver looked back before taking Piers' advice.

The girl looked up at Piers. "Is he ...?"

The man grunted and raised his head. He waved his gun feebly in the driver's direction. "Not police. Keep driving. Don't stop. No matter what."

"The guys behind us crashed," Piers said. "The police are on the scene."

"They'll kill the police and get another car. They won't give up until they get me."

The sound of an engine screaming grew behind them. The man looked at Piers with an I-told-you-so face. He grimaced as he wrenched himself into an upright position.

Piers kept low and looked to the rear. A police car was gaining on them. The man waved his gun drunkenly and fired.

Now he was in a gunfight with the police?

The police fired back and hit the man. He sank down until his face was level with Piers. His eyes drifted left and right then locked onto the small emblem on Piers' shirt. He grabbed it, yanking Piers close and wedging the gun under his jaw. Piers forced his tongue into the bottom of his mouth as if he could push away the gun.

The man's lower lip quivered. "Water ... loo." He shook Piers. "You idiot. They ... they ... th ..."

His head lolled and his grip on Piers' shirt was gone in an instant. The gun tumbled to the floor. A dark red stain spread from the center of the man's chest. His limp body sagged onto the rear seat, slid into the footwell, and slumped against the girl.

She screamed and wriggled out of the gap, her hands flapping at the man. "Get him off me!"

The driver turned around. "Is he dead?"

Piers saw the taxi veering toward the sidewalk. He opened his mouth to shout, but it was too late. He screwed his eyes shut as the car smashed into an old iron bollard on the side of the road. Piers' face hammered into the back of the passenger seat. His chest followed, crushing the breath from his body. Pain seared through his hips and shoulders. The girl's screams filled the car.

The rear of the car lifted off the ground, twisted around and came down onto a line of mopeds and motorbikes. The dead man's body lurched over Piers. He shoved it aside while the car still rocked on its suspension.

Piers could see the police car screech to a halt behind them. Two men in black suits jumped out, one a giant and the other completely bald. They were shouting, but Piers couldn't understand what they were saying.

He rolled out of his door. The girl was staring at him, her wide eyes pleading. He held out his hand. "It's okay. This way. They're police. We're okay."

She stared at him, her mouth half open, "No, no, not the police." She hurled herself out of the other side of the car, and ran.

The giant barked an order that sounded like Russian and the bald man rugby-tackled the girl, handcuffed her wrists, and dragged her toward the police car.

Piers moved toward her, reflexively.

The dead man was right, they weren't police. They must have been in the car that crashed and taken the police car, like the dead man said before they shot him. Maybe they thought he and the girl were involved with the dead guy.

He inched from the car. There was one motorbike left standing, its key dangling temptingly from the ignition switch. He'd never ridden a motorbike before, but he played Xbox and was an engineer, he knew how they worked. Throttle, gears and brake were all that mattered. Surely he could handle that?

He took a deep breath, stepped onto the bike and pushed it

forward. The kickstand snapped up and the bike bounced gently on its suspension.

The giant looked in his direction.

Piers smiled as he twisted the ignition key. The bike burst into life with an angry scream. His heart skipped a beat and his hands jerked away from the handlebars as if they were electrified.

Both men stared at him.

"Bonjour," called Piers.

He dipped the clutch, tapped the bike into gear, and twisted the throttle. The engine revved smoothly. He was surprised how easy it was, just like a video game. He was home free.

The giant brought up an enormous gun.

Piers ducked and twisted the throttle. The engine screamed and the bike shot forward, into the taxi. With a painful screech of metal, he scraped along the side of the vehicle, gripping the handlebar like a vice and swearing all the way.

The giant's gun thundered and automatic fire chewed up the bricks in the wall behind him, showering him with dust.

"We're innocent! We didn't know the man in the taxi!" Piers yelled, struggling to keep the bike upright. He squeezed the brake, and slid around the front of the car in a cloud of blue smoke, ending up facing the giant. "Don't shoot!"

The man leveled his gun. Piers ducked lower, pushing his elbows out and losing hold of the brake. The bike pitched up and raced forward, smoke pouring from its rear wheel. He squeezed his knees into the bike desperate to hold on. As he rode past the giant, his outstretched elbow caught the man in the jaw, punching him backward and launching his gun into the air.

"Sorry, sorry, sorry," Piers shouted, but he couldn't stop the bike.

The bald man threw the girl to the ground and yanked a gun from inside his jacket.

Piers' knees gave out and he slid off the back of the bike. He hopped along, gripping the handlebars until he finally caught the brake pedal with his foot. The bike toppled forward, wrenching him back onto the seat and flinging his legs out ahead of him. His heel smashed squarely into the bald man's chest, folding him up and hurling him backward over the police car.

The girl lay curled up on the ground. He brought the bike to a shuddering halt beside her and held out a trembling hand. He had to help her. His voice wavered with his pounding heart. "You ... you okay?"

She pulled herself up, swept her bound arms over Piers' head, and slipped onto the bike behind him.

He unclipped a helmet and held it out for her. As she waved it away, he glimpsed the giant scrabbling for his gun. "No, no. Don't. We're innocent. This is just a misunderstanding."

The girl slid her hand down Piers' arm and twisted the throttle.

"Nooooooooooo!" screamed Piers.

The bike weaved, its rear tire struggling for grip. The giant swung the gun toward them. Piers fought to keep his balance as they raced forward. The helmet felt like lead in his hand, before he could move it smashed into the man's face, flooring him.

Piers dropped the helmet, grabbed the handlebars and accelerated down the street, the front wheel in the air, the rear pouring smoke, and his heart in his mouth.

CHAPTER FIVE

Pierre "Matchstick" Morel gripped the telephone so hard it almost broke. He had gained his nickname partly because of his six-feet, 140-pound frame, and partly because he had a predilection for burning buildings. Usually the buildings of his enemies, and usually while his enemies were in them.

He forced himself to relax his grip on the phone, and breathed out a long hiss through his teeth. "What the hell do you mean, Auguste is gone?"

"There was shooting."

"Shooting? Who the hell was shooting?"

"Auguste, sir. He went mad."

"Auguste? If Auguste went mad then there was something bloody wrong. I should never have trusted that slimy dictator. He was there, non?"

"Who, sir."

"The dictator, you idiot!"

"Oh, yes, him."

"So, he was there?"

"No, sir."

"No? You said yes."

"No, sir. Well, yes, I did say yes, but no. No. No, he wasn't there."

"Listen. The fact that you and I share a great-grandfather is the one and only reason I'm not hunting for you with a can of gas. Get it?"

"Yes. Right. Sir. Yes. Got it ... Sir."

"Good. Now bring me the painting. I've already sold it for twice what I paid the dictator."

"Errrrr, Auguste had the painting, sir."

Morel rolled his head around, stretching his neck. "So? What's the problem? Tell Auguste to bring it to me."

"But, Auguste's gone, sir."

Morel stopped rolling his head around. "Gone where? Exactly?"

There was no reply.

"Where the bloody hell has Auguste gone?" he yelled.

"Gone as in dead, sir."

"Dead!"

"The dictator's men shot him."

"Shot him?"

"In a taxi."

"What they hell was he doing in a taxi?"

"We, er, we don't know, sir."

Morel breathed out, and regretted his decision not to send more men with more firepower.

"So, where's my painting?"

"Er..."

Morel leapt to his feet. "You don't know?" he yelled. He gripped the phone so hard his hand trembled. "I can't believe you screwed this up. I brought you in to keep watch on this operation. Nothing complicated. Just to keep watch."

"We did watch. The police were there, and there was lots of shooting, and we were gridlocked, and—"

"Spare me. You searched this taxi?"

"The painting definitely wasn't in it."

Morel groaned. "Can this day get any worse?"

"There's something else. There was a man and a woman in the taxi."

"Did they have the painting?"

"No. We'd have seen it when they left.

"You let them leave?" Morel's voice inched up an octave.

"Er, well, they were on a motorbike. They went off fast, clouds of smoke and—"

"You mean you lost them. The only lead we have and you let them get away. You slimy, good-for-nothing—"

"No, no, no. There's Auguste's phone, see. It's still moving."

Morel's face froze between anger and a sneer. "So?"

"Moving the same way the man and woman went."

"So, track them! Find them! Threaten them! Do whatever it takes, but find my bloody painting!"

"Yes, sir. Definitely, sir. No problem. We're on it."

"You better bloody had be. You've got twenty-four hours."

"And then?"

"I'll go all matchstick on them."

There was a small laugh. "That should do it."

Morel lowered his voice. "And on you, too. Understand?"

The man on the other end of the line swallowed hard. "Yes, sir."

CHAPTER SIX

"Slow down," the girl shouted in Piers' ear. "You're going to get us killed."

"They could be behind us."

"You shook them off a while ago."

"Why didn't you tell me?"

"I just did."

Piers eased up on the throttle. The engine groaning as it slowed.

"Go left here," she said.

"It's a one-way street."

"It's okay. I live up there."

Piers forced himself to relax, braked for the corner and turned into the street, ignoring the no-entry sign. A car horn blared and he veered for the gutter, narrowly missing a Ford heading in the opposite direction.

"How far?" he said.

"Not far. Maybe a mile."

"A mile! We could get arrested."

"Does James Bond worry about one-way streets?"

He avoided another car as it raced by, headlights flashing at them.

"No, but he's not real."

"Tell me about it. You try and get a guy to dress proper these days." She patted him on the shoulder. "No offense."

"Oh, none taken. I've been kicking myself all day for forgetting my tux on this trip."

"Right, see what I mean? Guys just don't want to wear nice clothes anymore."

Piers rolled his eyes. "Maybe it's because—"

The girl squeezed Piers with her arms and nodded toward a line of scooters by a café. "Stop over there."

Piers braked hard, almost throwing them both off, and lurched into the parking spot.

The café's patrons turned as one to stare at the interruption to their morning croissants.

She scissored her legs gracefully and twisted off the back of the bike, her arms still secured around Piers. He felt the patrons' stares leave the bike and focus on them as a couple.

The girl's face was inches from his. She gave a momentary smile, lifting her eyebrows. "Er ... um ... this is embarrassing, but could we ... possibly ... just walk? Casually? You know, like," she squeezed him, "arm in arm?"

Piers drew his head back. "Casually? Arm in arm? You're nuts! We've been shot at, crashed a taxi, stolen a motorbike, bloody near killed ourselves in these stupid narrow roads and—"

She smiled. Big. Broad. A thousand watts. "I know, and you were brilliant."

"I—"

She gripped him with her cuffed arms and kissed him full on the lips. Bold, brief, and hard.

His jaw hung slack and his eyes converged on a point inches in front of his nose.

She wrenched his numbed body off the motorbike. "Come on, before anyone sees these handcuffs."

He staggered, struggling to keep his balance. "What are we doing? Those people could catch up any moment."

"No problem." She dragged him to a pair of narrow double doors and barged through into an equally narrow hallway. Wallpaper curled from the ceiling and the painted woodwork hadn't been white for decades. A set of stairs ran upward. She took the first step and raised her cuffed hands over his head.

Piers grabbed her wrists. "Who were those people? How—"

She pulled free and held a finger over his mouth, "Sssshhh."

Piers quieted.

Her smile faded in an instant. "Good. Now, take the back door, go right, and down two blocks. There's a Métro station. You'll be okay then." Her smiled flashed and she turned to walk up the stairs.

"What? Wait!"

She jerked her head toward the rear door. "It'd be for the best."

"What would be? Have me walk out and get gunned down by some nutcase? Am I supposed to be some decoy—"

"Oh, don't be ridiculous."

"Ridiculous? I'm being ridiculous? You drag me into god knows what, get me shot at, and dump me who knows where, and I'm the one who's being ridiculous?"

"Ooohhh. You're English, aren't you?"

"What's that got to do with anything?"

Before she could reply, a door creaked and an old woman's voice called out "Who's there?"

The girl's pencil thin eyebrows narrowed. "Merde." She beckoned Piers frantically. "Up here. Now. Vite, vite."

"What? One minute it's so-long-and-thanks-for-all-the-fish and the next I have to follow your every instruction?"

"You're the one who's worried about nutcases, and this one's a doozy. What's more, you're a guy. She'll want a kiss."

Footsteps echoed on old floorboards. "Who is it? Who's there? Is that a man's voice?"

The girl gave Piers a told-you-so smile and bounded up the stairs. Piers followed, three steps at a time. On the third floor, the girl crashed into a door, fumbled the key into the lock, and swept inside. Piers dived after her and she swung the door closed, gently lowering the latch.

The girl leaned back on the wall and exhaled, long and slow. She rolled her head back and closed her eyes as she unbuttoned her jacket.

Piers' heart was pounding from adrenaline and exertion, but he couldn't stop his gaze from sinking down over the white blouse that fitted close across her chest and moved hypnotically with each breath, nor the short skirt wrapped tight around the very top of her long, toned legs. With a jolt, he realized she was staring straight at him. She lowered her face and he thought he saw her sneer for an instant. He flushed hot and his ears prickled. "I'm sorry, I, er, didn't mean ... I'm sorry ... who was that?"

She cleared her throat. "That?"

"The voice. The woman."

"Oh, right. That." She shrugged. "Landlady. Nosy so and so."

"That's not very nice."

"You haven't had to put up with her as long as I have."

Piers glanced around. It was a tiny studio apartment. A bed was pushed up against one wall and a cooker and sink were in the corner. A large armchair, a desk with a sewing machine, and a rolling rack of clothing filled most of the floor. Everywhere else, even the walls, were covered with bolts of fabric, fashion illustrations, sketches, and pages torn out of magazines. He whistled. "You've lived here a long time."

"Tell me about it. Since September."

"September?"

"September. The month I moved in. September."

"Which September?"

"This September. What is this, the Spanish Inquisition?"

"Sorry. I just thought you said you'd been here a long time."

"I have. I just told you. Since September. Five weeks. Five long weeks with nosy hounding me."

"That doesn't seem like a lo—"

Her eyes seemed to double in size. "It's a long time, all right?"

Piers put his hands up. "Okay, okay, it's a long time."

The girl pulled a tired looking cardboard box from underneath the sink, and produced a set of bolt croppers.

Piers stared. "You have bolt croppers?"

"There's no fooling you, is there?"

"Not every girl has a set of bolt croppers."

"Lots of people have them."

"Riiiiight. Do you often have to remove handcuffs?"

She stared at him and snorted. "Just cut the damn things."

Piers aligned the croppers carefully and squeezed. The handcuff gave in an instant. The girl wriggled and held up the other one, which was just as easily dispatched. She tossed the mangled metal on the bed.

She plucked jeans and a top from an open rack, disappeared into the bathroom and changed. She emerged, hung her original clothes on the rack, and smoothed down the fabric. Piers tried not to stare, but she looked no less fabulous in the second outfit than the first.

Under a pile of fabric on the armchair, she found a half-finished bottle of wine. The cork popped with a tuneful echo and she slugged a mouthful.

"Is that good?" said Piers.

She blew out a long breath. "Yeah. I needed it. I've been shot at."

"Me too, just in case you didn't notice."

"Yes, but they weren't really shooting at you."

"Weren't shooting at me? I nearly got my head blown off."

The girl gave a sarcastic smile. "Yeah."

Piers rolled his eyes at her and looked around the small room. "This is your apartment?"

She took another swig of wine. "Right on, Sherlock. What does it look like, a fish shop?"

"No. But people have been shooting at you and me, don't you think they might just happen to know where you live?"

"Why would they know where I live? This is a very good neighborhood."

"What's that got to do with anything? This is the first place they'll look."

"Trust me, this neighborhood is way too quiet."

"Quiet? It's not about the area being quiet, this is serious! We've been shot at. I mean, who were those people? What did they want?"

"I don't know! All right. All I know is they shot the guy who jumped into my taxi."

"*Our* taxi."

She scowled at him and took another swig of wine.

He took a deep breath. "All right. Where's the nearest police station?"

"Police? Didn't you see them shooting at us?"

"The police don't shoot people."

"Those ones did. Don't tell me you didn't notice."

"They weren't police. They were after the guy they shot. They probably think we're connected with him. That's why we need to go to a police station and tell them everything."

"But they waved guns and said, 'Halt, we're the police.' That's usually a sure sign. Plus, they were in a police car. So, no way, we're not going to the police."

"I didn't see any uniforms, and they weren't speaking French."

"Look, I know you're English, but not all police officers go around wearing silly hats and calling each other Bobby. And they must have been speaking French."

"They weren't. It sounded like Russian."

She stuffed the cork into the bottle, wedged it down the side of the sofa and walked to the kitchen area. "What did he say to you?"

"Who?"

"The dead guy."

"Oh. He called me an idiot."

She laughed loud. "You have to admit, he was a bit of a character."

"Character? He spat at me! And he used us as human shields."

She pulled a tub of ice cream from the fridge. "Oh, get over it. He didn't use us as human shields. What did he say before he called you an idiot?"

Piers scowled. "Something about Waterloo and construction."

"What was that about?"

"I work for Waterloo Large Construction."

"Oh, the people building down by the river?"

"Yeah."

"You don't look much like a workman."

"What's that supposed to mean?"

"You have clean fingernails and new shoes." She leaned forward and stared at his feet. "Correction, old shoes that have been polished. Still, not workman material."

She took a giant scoop of ice cream and slowly licked it off the spoon.

Piers wriggled in his seat, trying not to be mesmerized by her tongue. "We just need to get to a police station."

She shook her head. "No. No. No."

"Yes, yes, yes. Even if you don't want to go, I do."

She licked her spoon and flicked a tiny drop of melted ice cream at him. "You go, then."

He wiped the ice cream off his face. "Do you mind? Anyway, we both need to go. We need help. They can protect us while all this gets sorted out."

"You did see the bang, bang, the breaking glass, and the squealing tires? Please tell me you noticed that much?"

"That's exactly the point. The police will sort all this out."

"Really. A guy got shot in my," she huffed, "*our* taxi. There were bullets everywhere and you, very courageously I must admit, rescued me from a guy with a gun who was looking to shoot anyone who moved. What are you going to say? Sorry we were involved in a gunfight in the middle of the streets? A guy is dead, but we had nothing to do with it? The police probably think we killed the guy ourselves."

"They'll understand once we explain."

She rolled her eyes. "You don't know much about French justice, do you?"

He gave her a quizzical look.

"First they lock you up, then they send you to trial, then you have to prove you're innocent. Have you ever proved your innocence from a jail cell?"

"We won't be in a jail cell."

"Too right. After what just happened they'll shoot us on sight."

"They won't—" He sighed. "Either way, whatever we're going to do, we have to get out of here."

She shook her head. "Nah, dragon lady won't come up here. Doesn't like steps."

Piers rolled his eyes. "Not her! We've just been shot at by someone—"

"The police."

"Maybe—"

"Definitely."

He held up his hands. "Whoever it was—police, criminals, or whatever—they were after something, and probably still are."

"So?"

"I'm a visitor, but don't you think they might find out where you live?"

Her face froze and she stuffed the spoon into the tub of ice cream. "Well ..."

"Well nothing. We need to get out of here."

CHAPTER SEVEN

The girl piled out of her apartment and down the stairs, the ice cream tub tucked under her arm and the spoon in her mouth.

Piers caught up with her as she fumbled to open the front door. "What's your name?"

She looked back at him, "Who, me?"

He closed his eyes and shook his head in bewilderment.

She raised her eyebrows. "Oh, right. Sidney."

She peered out of the front door.

Piers did the same. "Don't you want to know mine?"

"Your what?"

"Name. Don't you want to know my name?"

"Oh. Yeah. Right. What's your name?"

"Piers."

She screwed her face up. "Like at the seaside?"

Piers sighed. "Yes, like at the seaside."

She stuck a spoonful of ice cream into her mouth. "Nice."

He didn't bother to clarify to which she was referring. "Which way to the police station?"

She shook her head. "Nah. We need to lie low for a while. I have a good friend. We can stay at her place."

"What friend?"

"You're all questions, aren't you?"

"I just want to know what I'm getting into. Do you know this friend well?"

"I just said so, didn't I? I met her in a bar. Last week. She's cool."

"Last week? In a bar? How can that be a good—"

She turned away, stepped out of the door, and began walking fast.

Piers rushed to keep up. "I still think we need the police, but where does this friend of yours live?"

"A few blocks away."

As they turned the corner, police sirens rang out. Piers grabbed Sidney's arm.

She flashed him a disgusted look. "Oh relax. You hear sirens all the time in Paris."

Three police cars screeched around the corner and raced down the street in their direction.

"Oops." Sidney stepped sideways into a small café.

The patrons paid them no attention as she chose a table for two at the back of the café. Piers squeezed into a tiny seat wedged in the corner. His skin prickled with sweat.

The police cars raced by and their wailing sirens receded.

Piers gave a great sigh.

Sidney raised her eyebrows. "See. Just because they had sirens on didn't mean they were coming for us." She scraped the last of the ice cream from the tub and pushed it to the corner of the small table.

The waiter arrived.

"Oh, er ..." She smiled at Piers. "Do you have any money?"

Piers rolled his eyes and ordered two coffees.

"I can't take this any longer. We need to go to the police," he said after the waiter departed.

Sidney shrugged. "How can we trust them? You saw what happened. We need to—"

A phone rang, a crude, old-fashioned buzz that reminded

Piers of his own ringtone. She rummaged in her handbag, pulled out a familiar looking, battered flip phone. She stared at the number on its small display.

"Wait." Piers eyes went wide. "Is that the dead guy's phone? You took his phone?"

"Well, it wasn't like he was going to use it, was it?"

"But that's evidence. Incriminating evidence. And now you've got it. We've got it."

"Oh, calm down." She looked at the number again and gave a disparaging grunt. "Don't know who they are. Not answering it."

"No wonder. It isn't your bloody phone."

"Okay, okay. I get it." She tossed the phone onto the table where it stopped ringing.

The waiter returned with the coffees. Sidney downed hers in one and handed the cup back to the man. "Great. I'll have another."

The waiter took the cup and stared. She smiled. "It was very good. Really. You should try some."

The waiter gave a haughty grunt and walked off.

Piers put his lip to the coffee, found it too hot, and put it back down. "Like I said, we need the police, at a police station."

He blew on his hot coffee.

The flip phone rang again. Sidney looked at the display without picking it up. "Merde. Same number."

"It might be someone wanting to know he's all right."

"So what am I going to tell them? Sorry, he's dead and I've got his phone?"

Piers shrugged. "You could play dumb."

She rolled her eyes, and flipped open the phone. "What?"

"I don't know what you think you're doing, but you're not going to get away with it." Piers could hear the other party's high-pitched male voice spilling from the phone's earpiece.

"Who's this?" said Sidney.

"Go to the police, and you and lover boy are going to be in deep trouble. Got it?"

"Lover boy?" said Sidney. She curled her top lip and stretched out the words.

"Don't get innocent with me. I know your sort."

"And what sort would that be?"

"Girls. I've dealt with girls before."

"Really? Fascinating."

"Not as fascinating as what Auguste was carrying."

"Who's Auguste?"

"The man whose phone you nicked."

"Oh."

"Oh, indeed, missy. You return what Auguste stole and maybe we'll let you go free."

"We're free at the moment, if you hadn't noticed."

The man was silent for several seconds. "Just return what you took."

"I don't know what you're talking about."

"Don't play stupid with me, missy. You're talking to an expert here. I mean ... I mean ... get us what we want and I won't have to set Gerard onto you."

In the background Piers could hear a deep voice. "I ... I thought we weren't going to use names?"

There was a high-pitched groan. "Well, that may or may not be his name, because you don't know. That could have been a ruse to make you believe it's his name when it isn't. Right."

"Riiiiight," said Sidney. "Look. I don't know who you are or what you're talking about, and I've got a lot of things on my mind at the moment, so I'm going to have to go." She lowered the phone from her ear. Piers grabbed it before the line went dead.

"Who is this?"

There was a laugh at the other end. "Ah, it's lover boy."

"I'm not anyone's lover boy, okay?"

"Ooohhh, touchy, touchy." The high-pitched voice sniggered.

"Look, if you're going to threaten us, the least you can do is explain what's going on."

The owner of the high-pitched voice cleared his throat. "Then listen up. If you don't return what Auguste stole within 24 hours, Matchstick Morel will be paying you a visit. And you don't want that, do you?"

"Who's Matchstick Morel? And we don't know this Auguste guy, so how are we supposed to know what he might have taken from you?"

"Pierre Matchstick Morel is a man you *don't* want to meet. And you know perfectly well what he took, so you better start looking. Speaking of looking, you better leave out the back, because some nosy old bat pointed you two out to those police guys who just raced past. And they're on their way to the café now."

Piers looked up. A knot of police officers stood outside. He grabbed Sidney's wrist and dragged her down a corridor that led to the kitchen.

She fought back. "What are you doing?"

"Police. Outside."

The waiter stood in front of them holding Sidney's coffee. She downed it in one mouthful as they pushed past.

They raced for the rear door. Piers hit it first, shoving down the emergency handle and tumbling out into a narrow, trash-filled rear lane.

"This way," said Sidney, racing to a featureless door on the opposite side of the road. She started hammering on the door. "Don't just stand there, get knocking."

Piers added his fists to the noise. "What are we doing?"

"This goes into a shopping area."

"Shopping?"

"There's a Métro station underneath."

The door opened. Sidney leapt forward, embraced a security guard, and gave him an exaggerated kiss on the cheek. "Thank god. We went out there by mistake and didn't know how to get back in. Oh, thank you, thank you, thank you."

She let go of the guard. "Got to run. Train to catch."

She bounded off. The guard turned his stare to Piers who shrugged and raced after her. To his relief, the guard closed and locked the door before there was any sign of the police following.

Sidney took a sharp left and bounded down a set of stairs, three at a time. Piers caught up with her at the bottom. "Where are we going?"

"One more floor to the platform." She pointed at a line of machines. "Tickets, quick."

Piers sneered. "Do you ever have any money?"

She stepped back. "You're going to argue about money at a time like this?"

He held his hands up in mock surrender. "All right, all right."

While he shoved euros into the ticket machine, she headed down the next set of steps, waving. He grabbed the tickets from the machine and ran after her. "Wait!"

Arms still waving, she turned right at the bottom of the stairs and disappeared from sight.

Piers leapt the last six steps in one go and crashed to the ground on a slick tiled floor. A platform full of people turned to look. He rolled to his feet and held up his hands. "I'm okay, I'm okay."

A presenter on an overhead TV babbled excitedly about a disturbance in Paris, but was drowned out by a train rolling into the station. He searched for the girl. "Sidney, Sidney!"

People on the platform backed away, opening a path in front of him. Sidney appeared, grabbed his hand and dragged him, stumbling, onto the train.

The people on the platform stared. Someone pointed at him. He knew he'd made a dramatic entrance onto the platform, but sometimes people were just weird. Sidney pushed him into a seat and wedged herself beside him.

He wiped his brow. "Nearly missed—" His gaze flicked from one person to the next. Half the subway car was staring at them. "What is ...?" he mumbled.

She wrapped her arm around his shoulder and pressed her mouth to his ear. “Shut up, and act natural.”

“What’s going on?” he said without moving his lips.

“Shut up,” she hissed. “We’re getting off at the next stop.”

The train slowed and entered a station.

Sidney grabbed his hand. “Okay, we’re leaving.”

The doors rattled open. She yanked him from the seat and bundled him out of the train. The platform was packed. A loudspeaker squawked arrival and departure times. Somewhere in the distance, he could hear the voice of another TV announcer.

“All right, I can manage,” he said, shaking himself free of her grip. “What’s going on?”

Sidney kept pushing him across the busy platform. He levered himself free. She grabbed him again. “Just keep going.”

The TV announcer’s voice seemed close. Piers looked up. A large yellow cube housed a small television with a badly distorted picture. A reporter with a microphone stood in a sea of police officers. “...less than an hour ago. He was pronounced dead at the scene.”

Sidney pushed. “Keep going.”

Piers stumbled a single step.

The TV camera panned back. Notre Dame came into view. “Oh no,” mumbled Piers.

“Keep going.”

“We were there,” Piers said.

“Full marks. Just keep going.”

The TV picture cut away to the view from a helicopter. A police car chased a taxi. The taxi crashed and two figures stumbled out of the rear, a man and a girl. The men from the police car drew guns and dived for the girl, forcing her to the ground and cuffing her. The man mounted a motorbike and swung it gracefully around the front of the car in a macho cloud of smoke and raw power.

Piers remembered how his heart had tried to jump out of his

chest when the bike started, and how it hadn't stopped trying until they reached her apartment.

The bike leapt forward, the rider felling a giant of a man with one blow, and kicking a second clear over their car. The smoke was still clearing as the rider lifted the girl onto the back of the bike as if she were weightless. The helicopter's perspective didn't show how she had helped, or how she had twisted the throttle to launch them down the street on one wheel and a cloud of smoke.

The helicopter lost the bike, but it didn't miss the men crawling back into the police car. Nor their zigzag departure after the couple.

"That was us," he said, without moving his jaw.

Sidney pushed against Piers' paralyzed form. "Can't deny that, but there's lots of people. Bad time to talk. Let's go." She pushed again, forcing him, stumbling, toward the opposite platform.

The announcer babbled excitedly about photo-enhancement. A train approached the platform, but Piers couldn't drag his eyes from the screen. People pushed forward, ready to board the train. He struggled to hear the words, but he couldn't miss the picture. The camera was frozen. Him on the bike. Sidney's arms wrapped around his chest. Only a thin arc of her dark hair poked from behind his head. He was gripping the handlebars of the bike, his terror looking for all the world like grim determination. The front wheel was off the ground, his leg outstretched, foot hammering the bald man in the chest. The camera zoomed in. He looked poised and purposeful, balancing the powerful bike as if he were born to it, a real-life James Bond.

The train stopped and the doors hissed open. The crowd waited mere seconds for the travelers to exit the carriages before surging forward. Sidney clung to his wrists. He stared into her eyes as the crowd squeezed them into the center of the carriage. He grabbed a pole for support. "That was us."

She gave a stupid grin, and a frantic shut-up-now nod.

Piers continued. "That was me. On the bike. Racing away."

Her smile softened. She tilted her head. "I know," she gushed. "It is a great picture." She ran a finger along the line of his jaw. "They really caught your features. You're lucky they got such a good angle. Not that you're bad looking ... Really ... I mean, you could do with a decent haircut and a little hair product. I hope they get a good shot of me, too."

"But I don't want to be on frigging TV."

Her smile vanished. "Keep your voice down."

"But—"

She clapped her hand across his mouth and dragged his ear to her mouth. "Shut up," she growled through clenched teeth. She pulled back and smiled. "Darling."

Piers' heart raced. He felt the weight of the people around him pushing. He tried to swallow, but his tongue stuck to the roof of his mouth.

What had happened? One minute he was talking to his mother and the next he was being shot at. Now he was on TV. It would be a matter of minutes before the BBC relayed the images. Then his mum, dad, friends, everyone would know it was him. He let go of the pole and wiped his palms on his jeans.

The train slowed with a lurch as they entered a station, and there was a push for the doors. They allowed themselves to be swept out and up the escalators with the crowd, with Sidney gripping his wrist tight the whole time.

They emerged into a fine drizzle. Sidney held her free hand over her head. "Great, this is going to ruin my hair."

"Who cares?" Piers said. "We've been shot at, watched a man die, been threatened by god knows who, and you're worried about your stupid hair?"

She glowered at him. "And they say old school British charm is dead."

"No, I meant ..."

Sidney walked off. "I know what you meant. You said it. My hair is stupid. Come on. I haven't got time to teach you manners. We've got to move."

Piers rushed to catch up. "Look, I meant after all we've been through, your hair is the least of our concerns."

"Least of your concerns, maybe. But me? I don't want to look like some tramp if they get my picture."

He grabbed her hand and stopped her. "Get your picture? Get your picture! This isn't a bloody game!"

Her expression hardened and she spoke through clenched teeth. "Keep your voice down."

"Keep my voice down? Keep my voice down?" He felt anger flash through his veins. He closed his eyes a moment and forced himself to take a deep breath. "All right, all right. We need to find somewhere quiet. Safe."

"Wow. No one can say your education was wasted. If you'd shut up and follow, I was on my way to somewhere safe."

She wriggled out of Piers' grip and walked on down the street. He rushed to keep up.

"I thought we were going to your highly trusted friend. The one you met in a bar last week."

Sidney smacked her forehead with the palm of her hand. "Well obviously that idea lost its appeal when the police turned up."

Piers ground his teeth and kept silent.

She took several turns and crossed numerous roads until they arrived at a large building with grand steps and tall columns outside.

"This is it?" he said. "This is your idea of somewhere quiet?"

She scowled at him. "Of course it's quiet. It's a library."

"We can't go in there and start talking without everyone noticing."

"Do you trust me?"

Piers raised his eyebrows. "No."

She hummed. "Well, try. Just for once." She walked in through the main entrance.

They took a narrow set of stairs that wound up to the third

floor. She threaded her way through the long rows of shelves to an alcove in the corner.

A statue of a mythical male creature stood on a dark wood plinth. Piers couldn't help but notice the creature was very well endowed.

Sidney elbowed him in the ribs. "It's Greek. They used to exaggerate things."

"You've been here before?"

Sidney beckoned him behind the statue. There was a half-height door in the wall with a plaque that said "Enfants Seulement." His eyes grew wide as she opened the door and ducked inside. He followed her into a small room.

Sidney flipped on the light, a single bulb dangling from a wire in the center of the ceiling. The walls were lined with books and posters. He saw images of Tintin, Asterix, and Jules Verne's sea creatures. In the middle of the room were two comfortable chairs and a coffee table. Small clouds of dust took flight as they sat down.

She leaned back and massaged her neck. "I used to come here with my parents when we were on vacation. Told them I sat here and read all day." She winked. "Actually, I used to stare at the statue a lot." Her grin faded. "Probably explains why my love-life has been such a disappointment." She sighed. "Anyway. I made a lot of friends in this room. Teenagers. We used to run around Paris. I found out how to ride the Métro for free, and places where you could pick up food, and ... well, then my father wouldn't bring me back because of the group I'd fallen in with. He didn't want me to grow up with a bad crowd."

"I'm glad to see his efforts weren't wasted."

Sidney screwed up her face. "Huh?"

"Never mind."

Concern evaporated from her face. "Anyway, we'll be safe here."

"That's a relative term."

Sidney grunted and lapsed into silence.

Piers hung his head down. "Those people at the station knew I was the person on the TV."

Sidney nodded.

"So, I can't show my face without people recognizing me."

Sidney nodded. "Maybe. Well, probably. Look, we should split up and get out of Paris until this blows over."

"Blows over? How do you think this is going to blow over?"

She shrugged and stood to leave.

Piers looked up. "Where are you going?"

"To stay with friends."

"And what I am going to do?"

"It'd probably be best if you went back to England."

"You think? Wow. Amazing how you come up with these ideas." Piers put his hand to his forehead. "And how am I going to get through customs when they have my picture?"

Sidney hummed then smiled. "Go to Spain. Or Portugal. You can get a boat back to England from there. Probably. They're not as strict with the passports, I don't think."

"And how am I going to get to Spain?"

She threw her hands up. "Am I supposed to think of everything?"

Auguste's phone rang, shockingly loud in the small space. She flipped it open. "What?"

Piers could hear the high-pitched voice again. Only this time it sounded different. Closer, more lifelike. "You two staying in there much longer?"

Sidney rolled her eyes. "Oh, glee. You found us again. Whoever you are."

"Never you mind who I am. When you've finished doing whatever you're doing in that room, I want to talk to you."

From outside the door Piers could hear a rumbling voice. "That should be we want to talk to you, not I. Because there's both of us here. You and me, and we both want to talk to them."

Piers let his head fall back into his hands, and sighed.

Sidney opened the door. Two men stood outside, one well

over six feet tall, in a dark three-piece and sunglasses, the other considerably smaller, in an ill-fitting light green lounge suit with a sheen. The small guy theatrically swiped his finger across his iPhone and placed it in his pocket. "So, you're done, eh?"

"Done?" said Sidney, her nose wrinkling up.

"With whatever you were doing in there." The guy sniggered like a ten-year-old girl reading dirty words in the dictionary.

Sidney stared at him.

His smile faded. "Oh, never mind. Get out here."

Sidney and Piers ducked out through the half height door. The big guy stood in the exit from the alcove and the small guy walked up to Sidney. He was a good six inches shorter than her.

She stared down at him. "So, you're the one who shot at us?"

The man stepped back. "Me? No. I didn't shoot at you. That was ... well ... that was someone else."

"Who?"

"Do you think I'm going to tell you that?"

"Why not? Wait a minute, how did you find us?"

The small guy gave a smug smile and leaned on the statue. "It's my business to know how to get hold of people."

Sidney nodded toward his hand. "I can see that."

The small guy looked at his hand. "Argh." He lurched away from the statue's exaggerated endowment. "Why do they have to do things like that? That's sick, that is. Sick. Suppose they think that's funny. So called artists."

"Terpsichore," said the large man.

"Terpsichore what?"

"The person who carved it."

"How do you know that?"

"There's a plaque here, see. Tells you all about—"

"All right, all right. I don't care." He turned back to Sidney. "What I want to know is, what are you doing to return what Auguste took?"

"We don't even know what he took."

Little's eyebrows inched closer together. "Don't play dumb with me, I'm an expert at that game."

"We've gathered that impression," Sidney said.

The small guy looked confused.

Piers stepped forward, took Sidney's hand, and led her around the man. "Okay, it's been nice talking, but we've really got to go now."

The big guy shuffled into the middle of the gap out of the alcove. He practically filled the exit. He grimaced and punched his right fist into his left hand, slow and firm. It made a loud smack. "I'm sorry, but you're going to have to return what Auguste took, or ..."

"Or?" Piers said, slowly.

"Or, we'll have to do this the hard way. And we don't want that. Not really." He winked. "Best to do it the easy way."

The small guy straightened his jacket. "So. You've got twenty-four hours, not a minute more. Got it?"

"We don't know anything about—"

The small guy walked away, his arm held high. "Talk to the hand." The big guy followed and in a moment the pair were lost in the rows of books.

Sidney blew out a long sigh. "That settles it. I'm going. I don't know who that pair are, or what they're talking about, but I don't like it. I'm getting a ticket straight out of Paris."

"What about me? I've been dragged round Paris by someone whose greatest concern is her hair, and now I'm on France's most-wanted list."

"Look, I know you've got your problems, but I've got to think about me."

"That's all we've done since we met."

"All we've done? When have you thought of me?"

"I don't know, let me see." Piers crossed his arms and rolled his gaze upward. "Maybe it was when I rescued you from the guys with handcuffs, or when I bought you coffee, or tickets at the Métro, or—"

"Oh, right, typical man. Just because you buy things you think that means you're thinking about me."

"Well, I bloody well have been!"

An old lady with a remarkable resemblance to an eagle stepped into the entrance to the alcove. "Do you mind? This is a library. If you wish to continue your shouting match, please do so outside, where I am sure you will be able to draw a larger audience."

She stood to one side. Sidney looked at Piers and gave an exasperated sigh. "Now look what you've done."

"Madame? Monsieur?" said the old lady, with one eyebrow raised.

Sidney stormed out and Piers assumed his usual role, following a few steps behind.

CHAPTER EIGHT

Piers took the steps outside the library two at a time, and caught Sidney by the arm. "We have to go to the police. You and me. It's the only way were going to sort this out."

She shook him off. "Don't be stupid. Look over there." She pointed at the two henchmen across the road. The small guy was sitting on a wall, his head almost at the height of the big guy and his legs dangling far from the ground. "If we go to the police, what do you think Little and Large are going to do?"

"Little and Large?"

She shrugged.

Piers couldn't deny the names were appropriate. "But what do you think they're going to do if you buy a ticket out of Paris?"

Sidney looked at Piers and her lips curled downward. "Oh." She sagged down onto the steps and wrapped her arms around her chest.

Piers sat beside her. "Yeah, oh."

"I only came here from ... well, I came here to show my designs. I only wanted a job. Just wanted someone to see what I could do."

"Me too."

"Huh?"

"I came here for a job."

"Well I'm not cut out for this. I can't deal with criminals and people threatening me. And look at you, you're not exactly James Bond."

"Thanks."

His phone rang, but it stopped before he'd fumbled it from his pocket. His mother's number glowed on the display. "Damn."

The small man across the road tapped his finger on his watch, and then drew his finger across his neck. For added effect he let his head flop sideways with his tongue hanging out.

Sidney stood up, said "Oh, oh, oh," and sat back down. "I've got an idea. Just play along."

"What?"

"You want to get rid of those guys, right? So, play along. Trust me."

Sidney rocked back and forth, and burst into tears, sobbing hard. "Me? Why me?" She sniffed. "Why me? Tell me? What have I ever done?" She raised her eyebrows, urging him to reply.

"I, er, I don't know."

She raised her voice. "I've always been good. I've tried my best. I always wanted to get a good job. I work hard. I'm nice to everyone. And then all this happens."

"Yes, it's, er ... terrible."

He noticed a group of women on the steps gesturing to Sidney, and turned his back to them as his phone rang. His mother's number glowed on the display. His finger hovered over the reject button until he remembered the TV pictures. Had they gotten to England already? Was his picture on the news as a wanted man? She'd be going nuts if she'd seen them. He pressed the green *talk* button.

"Hi, mum."

"Piers. I called a few moments ago. You didn't answer."

Sidney wrapped an arm around his neck and cried on his shoulder.

"I was busy, mum."

"Busy with what? And what's that noise?"

"It's nothing. Just things. You know. Stuff. Stuff to do."

"Well, I hope you're not getting into anything over there, dear."

Sidney snorted as she wiped her nose on her arm. "Why me? What have I done?"

"Piers, who is that?"

"No one, mum. It's nothing."

Tears streamed down Sidney's face. "I'm not a criminal. I've never hurt anyone. I haven't stolen anything."

"Stolen anything? Piers. What's going on there?"

"Nothing, mum." He struggled to disentangle himself from Sidney's arm and stand up. "It's nothing, really."

Sidney grabbed his wrist. "And I don't know anything about what that man took. I'm innocent. You have to believe me."

"Piers! What is happening? Have you fallen in with a bad crowd?"

"No, mum, no. It's ... it's ... it's the TV. Oh no, not the TV, it's not the TV."

"Piers! What on earth has gotten into you?"

Piers turned away from a middle-aged man in a jacket staring as he walked down the steps. "Mum. I wasn't trying ... I was just ... It was ..."

Sidney's sobs reached a crescendo. "Please, please. What have I done to deserve this? Why are they doing this to me?"

Piers shook off Sidney's grip. "I don't know—"

She grabbed his leg. "Don't leave me to them. I don't know what that man stole, or why they're following us."

Piers shook his leg. "Let go, will you."

"Piers! What an earth is happening? Who is that with you?"

Piers turned to see the middle-aged man kneeling at Sidney's side. "Can I help you, my dear?" She turned her sobs to him.

"Mum, I have to go. I'll ... we can talk later."

"Is this man hurting you?" said the middle-aged man.

Piers covered his phone's mouthpiece and glowered at the man. "I am not hurting her."

Sidney's sobs renewed in vigor and she grabbed the man's arm.

"Piers, we need to talk. If you're getting yourself mixed up in something, your father and I need to know about it."

"Mum. I have to go. I'll call you later."

"Piers! Don't you hang up on me!"

Sidney wailed.

The middle-aged man took hold of Sidney's arm. "Is this man abusing you?"

With a "Bye, mum," Piers mashed the off button, and wiped his brow.

Sidney shook the man's shoulder and sobbed on.

The middle-aged man took her hand and tried to steady her. "Are you all right, mademoiselle? Is this man hurting you?"

Sidney shook her head. "No. Not him. Over there." She pointed across the road.

The middle-aged man looked at an empty wall across the street. "What's over there?"

"Them." Sidney looked up and down the road. "Oh."

"Mademoiselle?"

"They were over there."

The man looked along the road. "Who was?"

Piers bent down. "It's okay, sir. We're okay."

Sidney shook Piers' arm. "They've gone."

"I know."

She blew her nose.

The man took her hand again. "Mademoiselle, are you all right?"

Sidney took a deep breath and swallowed. Her sobs evaporated. She put her hands on the man's arm and took a deep breath. "Oh, yes. Thank you for your help. Yes, you've been a wonder."

"Really?" His eyebrows crunched together so close they almost touched.

Sidney smiled, the full thousand watts.

The man blushed and eased to his feet. "Well, if you're sure, I'll be going then."

She smiled, and the man took to the steps, a definite spring in his stride. At the bottom, he turned to look back up. Sidney waved and he returned the gesture, a broad but quizzical grin on his face.

"I think he's going to start skipping," Piers said.

"He was a very nice man."

The group of women on the steps lost interest in Sidney and resumed their gossip.

"You faked all that."

"All what?" Sidney said with an innocent frown.

"All that. The tears, the wailing, the performance."

"Oh, that."

"Yes, that."

"Well, you were faking it talking to your mum." She wriggled her head as she emphasized "mum."

"I had to. I don't want her to worry."

"Don't want her to worry, yet you mention the TV?"

"I didn't think—"

"I told you that before."

Piers sighed. "So what were all the tears for?"

"I thought they might be sympathetic."

Piers stared at her. "Who?"

"Little and Large."

"Sympathetic? They're hit men. They not going to go back to their boss and say they let us go because you were crying."

"You really think they're hit men?"

Piers shrugged. "Maybe."

She sank back down and sat on the steps. "So, if we go to the police, they'll kill us."

Piers sat down beside her. "Probably."

"Definitely, more like." Sidney took a deep breath. "So what can we do?"

Piers shrugged. "Find whatever Auguste stole from them, I suppose."

"Damn."

"Yeah, damn."

CHAPTER NINE

Piers waited while Sidney fussed over her appearance in the reflection of a shop window. "God, I look awful."

She turned and looked at Piers. He had to admit her hair was a mess and her face was puffy from crying, but her eyes shone and her lips formed a wide line that bordered on a smile.

He smiled. "No, really, no ... you look nice."

She looked back into the glass. "Nice? Half a million years of human development and that's all you can say to cheer a girl up? Nice?"

"I'm not used to complimenting girls on their appearance."

She looked at him. "Apparently."

She fussed with her hair for a minute. "It's no good. I need something."

"What?"

"Something for my hair. What did you think I meant?"

"So, you want to shop for hair products while Little and Large plan how to bump us off?"

"The police are going to be looking for two people that look like they spent the morning on the run. And girls who don't have *nice* hair stand out in Paris. Do you want to stand out, Mr. TV star?"

Piers sighed. "Okay."

Sidney headed down the street to a pharmacy with a giant green neon cross in the window. The shop appeared full of middle-age women loading up on creams and lotions promising youth.

Sidney examined an unending string of brightly decorated bottles. Piers stood at the end of the isle, shuffling his weight from foot to foot, and furtively glancing at the security camera in the corner. If anyone figured out who they were, the police would have an even better picture of him, and a good picture of Sidney. She was safe until they got a good shot of her. He bit his lip and willed her to find something and get out fast.

She examined the small print on a florescent purple jar. "You don't have to stand all the way over there. I'm not buying feminine products."

"Huh?"

"Feminine products."

Piers placed his finger over his mouth and shushed her.

Sidney shook her head. "I'm not buying feminine products."

Piers' brow furrowed "What feminine products?"

She plucked a box of tampons from the shelves and tossed it at him. "Feminine products. I'm not buying feminine products."

He missed the catch and the box crashed into the lady who stood next to him, who was reading the advertising on a product that claimed to give a "youthful glow." He fumbled an apology as she moved to another aisle.

He grabbed the box from the floor and waved it a Sidney. "Okay, so what?"

"So you can stand next to me. I'm not contagious and I'm not going to embarrass you."

"Really?" Piers pushed the tampons into an empty space between two brands of shampoo. He walked over to her. "Better?"

She smiled. It was a warm and inviting smile, one that every woman in the shop would likely have killed for. Piers swallowed and half-smiled back, his eyes and cheeks anesthetized, but his lips spread across his face. She laughed. "You're weird."

"Thanks."

A stern voice sounded behind him. "Do you need these, sir?"

He turned to see a shop assistant in a white lab coat shaking the box of tampons in front of his face. "Do you need these, sir?"

He shook his head slowly.

"Then please return the products you do not wish to purchase to their proper location."

The assistant brushed him aside, placed the box amid a large display, and stomped off.

Sidney raised her eyebrows and grinned. "Oops."

Piers frowned. "Have you found something yet?"

Sidney waved a small black jar with a bright orange wavy stripe at him. "Let's go."

They lined up at the checkout. Sidney paid with a twenty-euro bill and shoved a handful of change back in her pocket. On the way out of the store, she stopped at a mirror and fixed her hair with a brush. When she turned around she looked stunning. The perfect wave of her relaxed curls had been restored. Every strand of hair was artfully arranged, and the left-hand side was perfectly flipped over her ear. She grinned and lowered the tone of her voice. "Better?"

Piers smiled and licked his lips. "Amazing."

Her grin turned into a contented smile. "Well, that's an improvement." She patted his arm. "Who would have thought? From nice to amazing with one jar of hair goop."

Piers led out of the shop and noticed Little and Large on the opposite side of the road. Large wore wrap-around sunglasses over an impassive face, but Little had a gloating grin and tapped his watch.

He wondered if they should confront them again. Find out something about the guy who had been shot, and what he was supposed to have stolen. He'd barely said a word before he was shot. They didn't have a clue about—

He turned to Sidney. "Do you still have the guy's phone?"

Sidney nodded.

"Good, let's get a coffee."

They took a table in the back of a small café. She handed over the battered mobile phone.

The waiter arrived and Sidney ordered two coffees, a wallet in her hands.

Piers stared at her.

She pinched her eyebrows together. "What?"

He shrugged. "I thought you didn't have any money."

Sidney covered her wallet with her hands.

Piers mouth hung open. "Wait a minute." He grabbed for the wallet, but Sidney was quick and tucked it into a pocket.

Piers leaned forward. "You took his wallet, didn't you?"

"No."

"Well, what was that?"

"What?"

"The thing you just hid."

"Mine."

"Your wallet?"

"Of course."

"Didn't look like a girl's purse."

"I prefer a wallet."

"Really?"

"Yes, really."

The waiter returned and thumped two coffees on the table. He stared at Piers.

He nodded at Sidney. "She's paying."

She fumbled in her bag, keeping it under the table, and produced a twenty-euro note. The waiter rummaged in his pockets, cheerlessly dumped her change on the table, and left.

Sidney scooped it up and dropped it into the wallet. Piers got a clear view this time. It was light tan, worn thin, but clearly leather. Equally clear was a big red stain. "Nice decoration."

Sidney bit her lip and lowered her gaze. She turned it over in her hands. "He wasn't going to use it, was he?" She licked her lips. "I mean, I don't think he'd mind."

Piers shrugged. "Hard for him to express an opinion now, isn't it?"

Sidney gave a big sigh. "Look, I'm not proud, but I haven't had any money for days. Do you know how expensive it is to live in Paris?"

"Believe me, I'm learning."

Piers leaned back and took a sip of nearly cold coffee. "I should be mad ... but what's in it?"

"I haven't looked."

Piers slapped his forehead. "Well, let's not worry about sorting out the mystery of who this guy is, and what he did."

Sidney glowered. "All right. It's not like I've had a lot of spare time." She pulled the money out and dropped the wallet onto the table. "You search it."

Piers stared at it for a moment. At least it had landed blood-side down. It didn't look ominous. It wasn't a valuable possession, not something someone rich and powerful would have. Not that someone rich and powerful would have been running from gunmen. They'd have been sipping martinis and assembling their lawyers from their penthouse suite. No, this wasn't the wallet of someone who sipped martinis.

He picked it up and turned it over. The ugly red stain ran across one side like a river, twisting and turning, changing direction under the influence of invisible forces. One corner was frayed and he toyed with a thread that was unraveling before looking inside. There were five credit cards and a wedge of credit card slips. He pulled them out.

The cards were standard fare: Visa and MasterCard, but no gold cards. "Auguste Chevalier," he said.

Sidney stared at him. "Does that help?"

Piers shrugged and went back to examining the wallet.

The paper slips were from various automated machines. Piers sorted them into piles and found equal-sized transfers from one card, to a bank, to another card. They weren't big amounts, a few hundred euros, but clearly the man had been jugging his debt.

"Nothing personal in—"

He stopped to look at two small pieces of thin card that Sidney was waving in front of him.

"They were mixed in with the money," she said.

He reached for them, but she drew them away. "Say please."

He sighed and held his hand out. "Please."

She looked at him with mock seriousness. "Say, well done, Sidney, for finding out about Mr. Chevalier."

"Just give me them, would you?"

She raised her eyebrows.

He forced a smile. "Please."

She handed over the cards with a grin.

Piers flipped them over. "Train tickets."

"Boy, you're a genius."

"To Milano."

"Milan," she said.

"Boy, you're a genius."

She stuck her tongue out at him and turned away.

"Damn." Piers jumped up, grabbing the wallet and its contents and shoving them in his pockets. "We've got to go."

"Why?"

Piers waved the tickets. "This train leaves in twenty minutes."

"So? He's not going to be catching it. He's dead."

He waved them again. "*Two* tickets."

CHAPTER TEN

Piers pounded up the steps from the Montparnasse-Bienvenüe subway to the railway terminus above. Sidney was a good flight of steps behind him shouting for him to stop.

According to the station clock they had seven minutes to find Auguste Chevalier's traveling companion. He surveyed the monitors and found the Milan train.

Sidney staggered to his side, doubled over, and grabbed a railing. "When I said stop, I really meant stop."

He patted her on her back. "You're doing great. Come on. Platform four."

"Platform nothing. I have cramp in my side. I can't move."

Piers hooked his arm under hers. "Come on, we can't split up."

She wriggled, but he kept a firm grip and dragged her toward platform four.

She thumped his back. "Let go before I call rape."

Piers stopped and let her go. She massaged her side and eased herself upright. "For your information, that hurt."

Piers nodded. His shoulders slumped and the muscles in his face relaxed downward. "Sorry. Really. But the train leaves in six minutes."

Sidney grunted and rubbed her stomach. "All right, action man. Go on."

They hurried to platform four, passing several railway employees who were more interested in their lunch destination than checking passenger tickets.

"How are we going to find this person?" Sidney said, still holding her side.

"Easy. They haven't got a ticket, so they'll still be here when the train leaves."

Piers slowed his pace. A train sat idling, but a mass of people stood waiting, their luggage beside them. Small shops ran along the rear of the platform. Stairs led up to a balcony that ran the length of the shops and gave access to offices above. Sidney pointed to the departure board. A second train was scheduled to leave from the same platform, ten minutes after the Milan train.

He rubbed his forehead. "Great, so we don't even know which train these people are waiting for."

"Who do you think it might be?" Sidney said.

Piers shrugged. "A woman?"

Sidney hummed and looked around the crowd. "Maybe. He could be married."

"You didn't nick his ring then?"

"Huh?"

"You didn't take his wedding ring?"

She glowered at him, her eyebrows pressed down hard. "He didn't have a wedding ring."

"So, you did check?"

She shook her head angrily. "Women notice these things. Unlike men who think they're just a decoration."

"Right."

Occasional people joined and left the platform, a sandwich seller did a brisk business in baguettes, but no one stood out as Auguste's companion.

"It might be a he," Sidney said.

"Maybe."

"We're not really getting anywhere. Perhaps we should just walk up and down calling out his name."

Piers turned his attention from the crowd to Sidney. "You think someone's going to answer us? The guy was obviously doing something bad, and has tickets to leave town in a hurry. Whoever it is, they're hardly likely to put their hands up, now are they?"

Sidney grunted. "So what's your plan?"

"I—"

The phone in Piers' pocket vibrated. The sound of the ringer was muffed but persistent.

"You going to answer that?" Sidney said.

"I don't care. It's probably just the office."

"You have the same ring tone as the dead guy?"

Piers thrust his hand into his pocket, grabbing for the phone and pulling it out. He flipped it open and the ring tone stopped. "Bugger, missed it."

He pressed a few keys and found the missed call list. "April."

"April, what?"

"The call was from someone called April."

Piers looked at the station clock. Three minutes before the train was scheduled to depart. "Maybe his companion is getting worried."

April's number still glowed on the display. He placed his finger over the redial button. "Spread out, see if anyone's phone rings."

Sidney pushed her way through the people on the platform. Piers knew this was going to be a long shot. There were a lot of people and even if they could hear a phone ring they'd only have seconds to locate the person. He took a deep breath and pushed the button.

There were a few moments of agonizing silence, then clicks, then the earpiece started to give a ringing tone. He looked around and saw Sidney doing the same. There was no telltale phone sound, and no one was rummaging in their pockets or handbags. He moved the phone back to his ear to hear a whistling sound. The call hadn't gone through.

The clock said two minutes to go. He pressed redial. There was the same silence, the same clicks, and the same ringing. Only this time a shrill *chirrup* joined in. It wasn't coming from the earpiece, it was on the platform. It was April's ringtone. He looked all around, his eyes and ears searching. He glimpsed Sidney doing the same. Whoever it was had to be between them. He pushed through the crowd, his eyes scanning left and right. The noise seemed close, but no one was answering a call. Sidney was closing in too. They made eye contact. She shrugged.

He heard a voice on Auguste's phone and whipped it to his ear. Then he heard the same voice nearby. April had to be close, but still no one was moving. He looked straight up. A woman stood on the balcony. As if by psychic connection, she looked down at the same instant. Their eyes met. Without words or facial movements, she knew she had blown her identity, and Piers knew he had found her. She was running in an instant.

Sidney had spotted her, too, and was running for the steps at the far end of the platform. Piers took the steps closest to him. April couldn't get off the balcony without passing one of them, but there were plenty of doorways adjoining the balcony, and April took one.

In a moment, she reappeared and took the next doorway. Piers ran hard, but it looked like Sidney would reach April first. Piers' skin prickled. April was Auguste's partner in crime. The man who had been shot in their taxi. The man with the gun. And if he had a gun, would she?

"Sidney! Stop! Wait there!"

Sidney didn't stop.

Piers ran harder, waving his hands. "Stop! Sidney!"

Sidney skidded to a halt by the doorway April had taken and stood very still. Piers was only paces away from the doorway. He stretched his arms out and barreled into Sidney, sweeping her up and away from the opening. She gave a scream, and he managed a couple of paces before he lost his grip and his footing. They went down in a jumble of arms and elbows on the hard floor. He rolled off her and up onto his haunches, bracing himself for the sight of a weapon.

She lay on the floor. “What was that for?”

“She has a gun.” Piers grabbed Sidney’s hand and started pulling her up.

Sidney wrestled out of his grip. “No, she bloody doesn’t”

Piers stopped mid-grab for Sidney’s arm. “She doesn’t?”

April was back on the balcony. He shoved Sidney aside and lunged for April. The woman stepped left, but Piers caught onto her big coat and manhandled her back into the doorway.

She twisted uselessly. “Get off me or I’ll scream.”

“We need to talk to you.”

“I don’t care. I’ve got a train to catch. Let me go!”

“We came to tell you why Auguste’s not here.”

April’s expression froze for an instant, a brief stutter in the film of her life. “I don’t know what you’re talking about. I’ve got to go.”

Piers relaxed his grip. “He’s dead.”

He felt a smack on the back of his head and Sidney pushed him aside. “For god’s sake, is that the best you can do?”

April put her arms up in front of her face. “I don’t know who you’re talking about. I have to go.”

Sidney touched her arm. “We really need to talk to you.”

The train gave a long blast of its horn and the passenger doors slammed shut.

“That’s my train. I should be on it.”

“We know. We’re sorry.”

The train’s engine roared and the floor trembled faintly as it pulled out of the station.

April didn’t move. “I should be on that train. It’s my train.”

Sidney put her arm around her. “We know, we know.”

“Auguste’s just late. He’s just late.”

Sidney gave a slight shake of her head.

April looked at her, her eyes imploring, "He's never late. I know him. He's dependable. Always. He must be stuck in traffic."

Sidney shook her head again. "He jumped in my taxi a couple of hours ago."

"No."

"Yes. He was injured."

"No ... no ... no, he wouldn't have been in a taxi."

"He was," Piers said.

April kept shaking her head. Tears welled up in her eyes, and she sniffed.

"He'd been shot," Sidney said.

April's head shaking grew more forceful. "No. You're wrong. It couldn't be. Not Auguste."

"Yes."

"He was going to meet me here."

"We know."

"He couldn't have been in a taxi."

"He was. He was being shot at. They shot at us too."

"No."

"It was the police," Sidney said.

"Might have been the police," Piers said.

Sidney gave him an angry glance before giving April a squeeze. "We were there. He died in the taxi."

April pawed at the collar on Sidney's jacket. "But he wasn't supposed to be in a taxi. That can't be right. He's just caught in traffic. He'll be here." She bit her lower lip. "Won't he?"

Sidney and Piers shook their heads in unison.

Tears poured down April's face. Her mouth hung half open and her bottom lip stuck out, trembling. Sidney pulled her close while she wept. Piers patted her on the back as he looked up and down the platform. There was no one suspicious, no police, no Little, and no Large. Maybe they were ahead of the game.

He looked back at Sidney, only to find her glowering at him. "What?" he mouthed.

She rolled her eyes and patted April's back.

"We need to keep a look out," Piers said. Sidney gave him a disgusted glance.

April pulled a tissue from her pocket and wiped her nose. "What happened?"

"We were in a taxi. He jumped in."

"No, he wouldn't."

"He did. People were shooting at him."

"There shouldn't have been ... no ... he wouldn't have been in a taxi."

"All we know is he jumped in our taxi."

April blew her nose. "So how did you find me?"

Piers pulled the wallet from his pocket and held up the train tickets.

Sobbing, April took them. She ran her finger down the line of the blood on the leather. "Are you police?"

Sidney shook her head.

"Then why do you have this?" April held up the wallet.

"We took it," Sidney said.

April's eyebrows narrowed. "You took it off my Auguste?"

Sidney hesitated then nodded.

April put her hands around the wallet. "You took it from him when he was dying?" She shoved Sidney backward. "You stole it. You're a thief. You're a con ... you, you ... maybe you killed him."

"No, no. He jumped in our taxi. He was injured."

April turned to Piers. "You had his phone. You took his phone. You must have killed him."

"No, the men he was running from were shooting at us. They killed him. They did."

"You used his phone."

"To find you."

April's face jerked and contorted, a slow dance of pain and grief. "No, no, no."

Auguste's phone buzzed in Piers' pocket. As he reached for it, April launched a punch. She hit him at the base of his ribs. He didn't think it was going to hurt but the pain welled up through his lungs and down through his stomach. He gripped his side and stumbled backward, crashing into the railing overlooking the platform.

April ran.

Sidney took off after her.

Piers fumbled Auguste's ringing phone from his pocket. "What?"

It was Little's high-pitched voice, but without a hint of his sarcastic tone. "Don't know what you're doing up there, but you might want to leave quick. You've got company. The police are heading your way."

CHAPTER ELEVEN

Piers heard Sidney calling for April to stop. He watched the pair come to a halt a short distance from the steps. For a moment, he was relieved that April appeared to be heading back, but it was only a moment, because a line of gendarmes appeared at the top of the stairs.

"Find a way out!" Sidney shouted as she sprinted toward him, April a pace behind.

He forced himself up and worked from door to door until he found an open one that led to a staircase.

"Go!" yelled Sidney as she arrived at the door.

He didn't need further prompting. He headed up the bare concrete stairs, three at a time.

On each floor, he slammed into the exit doors, but they were locked, designed only to be opened from the other side. Sweating, he reached the top of the stairs. He hammered on the last door while crushing his face against a small wire-reinforced porthole and peering left and right. Beyond the door, he saw a plush corridor with an old painting of the station and its famous train wreck dangling from the second floor. Sidney joined in hammering on the door.

"They're on the steps," April said.

Piers started kicking the door to make more noise. A waiter's face appeared at the window. Sidney pressed her face up to the porthole, screamed help, and implored him with her eyes. The door lock clicked in an instant.

Piers shoulder-barged the door. It flew open, smacking the waiter in the face and sending Piers stumbling into the far wall. Sidney and April were right behind. Sidney slammed the door. They were in a corridor with imposing entrances at either end.

The waiter rubbed his face. "Madame et monsieur, the entrance is at the next stairway." As he pointed to a grand door at the end of the corridor it swung open, and two police officers rushed through.

"We've got to go," Piers said.

The officers shouted for them to stop. Piers grabbed Sidney's hand and ran in the opposite direction down the corridor. He heard April's shoes thumping behind him. He ran through an archway, and they stamped into an ocean of tranquility. A thick carpet padded gently underfoot. The walls were decorated with a dark, velvet wallpaper and gold-framed paintings. Spotlights picked out intimate tables. In uncanny unison, the diners at those tables turned to look at them.

"Excuse us," Sidney said, as she dodged her way through the well-dressed patrons toward a pair of swing doors on the right side of the room. April followed and Piers brought up the rear. A rotund maître d' barreled in their direction. As they passed through the swing doors, Piers grabbed a mop and wedged it into the door handles. The maître d' bounced off the doors, then returned with a booming voice, demanding to be let in.

Steam rose from pots and pans all around a tiny kitchen. There was no other exit. Three cooks were packed into one corner, apparently tasting something. After a moment's surprise, they armed themselves with pots and pans.

"We don't mean you any harm," Piers said, holding up his hands.

"Get out," said the head chef.

"There's a man after us."

The chef advanced on them. "Then call the police. Get out."

Sidney opened a small hatch in the far wall. "Over here."

April and Piers danced around the cooks to join her.

The head chef folded his arms and smiled. "Go ahead. It's only five floors straight down into the trash."

Sidney grabbed a tablecloth from a pile on a cart. She held it out to April. "Wrap it around your feet and back. Press on either side of the chute to slow you down."

Her eyes widened. "Me?"

There was a hammering on the door. Piers saw a flash of police uniform through the small window. "Yes, you. Unless you want to deal with them."

April wriggled into the opening and wrapped the sheet round her legs. "This is stupid."

"Go!" said Sidney, wrapping another tablecloth around herself.

One of the cooks started for the door.

"Wait," said the head chef. "This I have to see."

April dropped into the chute, screaming.

The chef nodded. "I'm impressed. Now open the door."

Piers grabbed Sidney and stepped into the hatch. He forced his feet against one side of the chute and his back against the other. His shoes skidded and juddered on the smooth metal. Sidney rolled into a ball in his arms and they rocketed downward. His back grew hot and he couldn't see below, but above them he could hear shouting. The outline of someone appeared at the hatch, but in a moment, they were gone.

"Hope they don't have a bloody gu—"

Piers' feet flipped off the end of the metal, and his back fell away under Sidney's weight. He redoubled his grip on her and curled his head forward, cringing.

The ground wasn't what he had expected. They hit it with a percussive *whump*. It was soft, trash bags filled with god knows what. The plastic was almost frictionless, and he slid sideways.

The impact on his back felt more like a mistimed jump into a swimming pool than a concrete floor. The smell wasn't what he had expected either. A savory, sickly sweet putridness. He almost gagged.

Sidney struggled to get free. He relaxed his grip and she levered herself off him by wedging her elbow in his stomach. He struggled to get up on the squirming bags.

The room would have been pitch dark but for the glow from April's mobile phone. She was searching the walls. "This was a stupid idea."

Piers snorted. "Did you want to see if we could talk our way out of things with the police?"

"You didn't even look for another way out!"

"There wasn't another way out. Didn't you notice the guys with the pots and pans and the police at the door?"

"Don't be stup—"

"Stop it," shouted Sidney. "Both of you. We need to get out of here."

Piers clenched his teeth, and took out his phone for illumination.

"There's a crack down the corner of this wall," Sidney said.

Piers scrabbled over the stinking bags and saw the line of light in the corner. There was a gap. He ran his phone upward. The gap went right to the top of the room then along the ceiling. "The whole wall's a door. We need a lever or something."

"Here," April said from the other side of the room.

"Pull it," Piers and Sidney said in unison.

April put her weight onto the lever. There was a metallic crunching sound, a rumbling, and light burst in through the top of the wall. It shook and rattled like an ancient drawbridge.

The wall opened onto a parking area for a trash truck. Piers expected to see a line of police officers, but there were none. Beyond the parking spot, pedestrians and Paris traffic bustled. Piers stepped forward as the door headed for the horizontal. They were still high above the ground, the trash was obviously poured straight into the rear of a parked truck. The floor began to tilt.

Sidney screamed and grabbed his arm.

"Jump!" He said.

He leapt down to the ground. His feet stung from the impact but he turned just in time to adsorb the weight of Sidney landing in his arms. He rolled her to one side and shuffled right to catch April. But April didn't jump. The bags started rolling and sliding from the filthy floor. Piers leapt back, and April was deposited gracefully down on a mound of garbage. Piers pulled her off.

Sidney was already looking up and down the road. She jumped out into the traffic, zigzagged to the middle lane, and stepped in front of a taxi. Piers dragged April through the traffic as he listened to screeching tires and prayed Sidney wasn't hit. When he reached the taxi, she was already in the passenger seat. Piers followed April into the back. The taxi driver screwed up his nose and rolled down the windows.

"Charles de Gaulle. Move it, we're late," Sidney said. The taxi eased off and joined a line of traffic.

Piers leaned forward. "Fifty euros if you get us there on time."

The taxi driver grunted and swung the car, tires squealing, into the oncoming lanes, and accelerated away.

Piers looked at April. She had her hands on her lap and her head down. She was biting her lip. He patted her shoulder. "We'll be all right."

She took deep breaths. "But he won't, will he? It's not like you can do anything for him, can you? You're just going to walk away and live your lives."

Piers sighed. "I know we can't help him. But now we're in danger because of him."

She scoffed.

"The people who were chasing Auguste think we have something he took."

She gave a derisive snort and raised her eyes to him. "And

what am I supposed to do? Maybe you work for them. Maybe you killed him?"

"We didn't kill him."

"So you had someone do your dirty work."

"We were bystanders to whatever happened and now we're being threatened with our lives."

She snorted. "That was the police back there. Why didn't you tell them?"

Piers sighed. It was a good question.

She gestured behind them with her hands. "Really. Go and tell them."

He took a deep breath. "We can't. We think they shot at us as well."

"The police?" asked the driver, looking at them through the rearview mirror.

Sidney slapped the driver on the shoulder. "Just watch the road."

April had her head down and looked at Piers from the top of her eyes. "You can't trust the police?"

"Maybe, maybe not. It was hard to tell. There was a lot of gunfire."

The driver's face appeared in the rearview mirror. "The shooting on the radio. You were there?"

"Do you mind?" Piers said, "Just drive."

"But they've been talking about it. Bunch of people been shot at Notre Dame. Gare de l'Est, too."

"Gare de l'Est?" Piers said.

"According to the radio. Criminals. They said some survived."

April's head shot up. "Who?"

"Who what?"

"Survived, for God's sake."

The driver shrugged. "I don't know. Some of them. That's all they said."

April grabbed the driver's shoulder. "We need to go there. Now."

Piers eased April back into her seat. "We saw him. We were in the same taxi."

"I don't care. Some of them survived. He said so. He said it's been on the radio."

Piers shook his head.

She stared at him, long and hard. "You're sure."

He nodded.

"Are we still going to the airport?" the driver said.

Sidney slapped him, harder this time. "Just shut up and drive."

April sank into the corner of the rear seat, and sobbed. Sidney tapped Piers on the shoulder and mouthed, "I should have sat in the back." Piers couldn't help but agree. The last thing he wanted was to deal with a crying woman. They emerged from the confines of Paris' buildings and crossed the Seine. "Where are we?"

Sidney glanced along the river. "Austerlitz."

"Which is?"

"A bridge."

"Where?"

Sidney pointed. "Notre Dame's over there."

"Okay. We'll get out here."

"Here?" said the driver.

Piers glowered. "What is this, twenty questions? Yes. Here. Stop here."

"Okay. Only you said the airport."

"Well, we've changed our minds."

"You said I'd get a tip."

"Whatever."

The taxi drew to a halt beside a line of cafés. Sidney eased April out of the taxi while Piers handed over the fare and promised tip.

Sidney wrapped her arm around April. "We should go somewhere quiet."

Piers looked at the pair. "Let's sit down for a minute, have a drink."

"We stink," said Sidney. "Big time."

"We'll sit outside. No one will notice."

Piers found a free table in a quiet corner. They seated the silent April and angled themselves to have a view of the street. April kept her head down.

A waiter arrived, his nose screwed up to hold his breath. Sidney ordered three large brandies.

Piers ducked his head down to get into April's line of sight. "We need to know what Auguste was involved in."

She shook her head. "He was a good man."

"I'm sure he was, but we need to know. Our lives are in danger."

She sat silent, and the waiter returned with the drinks. Piers could smell the brandy over their own stench. He handed over a twenty. "Keep the change." It seemed only fair given their condition.

Sidney persuaded April to take a drink. She took a couple of sips then downed the glass in one.

Piers gave the alcohol a moment. "April, we really need to know about Auguste."

She gave the barest of nods. "He liked to joke about things. That's how we met, how we got to know each other. You know, Auguste and April, we've heard all the jokes."

Sidney placed her hand on April's shoulder, and April placed her hand on top. "I knew what he did from the moment we started going out. I knew it was dangerous. And ... and not always right. But he wasn't bad. Not really. He didn't use guns." She drew herself up. "I don't know about the shooting. He wouldn't," she shook her head, "he didn't. No. Not Auguste."

Sidney squeezed her hand. "But what was he doing?"

April put her hands together in her lap. She gave Sidney a sideways glance, then looked down at her hands. "You have to understand. Auguste worked for the same man for ten years. We struggled to pay the rent some months. It wasn't easy. His mother, my father, they were old, they needed looking after. And his boss was so rich. Money for anything. And always Auguste helped, never complained. When Auguste's mother passed away, we talked about doing something different, but how could we? We didn't have the money. When my father passed ... then we knew we had to do it. To do something. A new life. A fresh start." She wiped her nose on her sleeve. "This was going to be it."

"So you were running away?" Piers said.

April rolled her eyes. "We knew we couldn't stay in Paris. We'd lived our whole lives here, and all we owned was an old car that he worked on every weekend just to keep going."

She looked up at Piers and he nodded sagely, hoping she would get to the point soon. "And?"

"And we had to do something. He wanted to do something. He was good at things. Good at listening, good at figuring things out."

"What did he figure out?"

She bit her lip. "There was a painting. Valuable. He figured out about the painting."

"What painting?"

She rubbed her hands together. "I don't know. He planned things. On his own. He said the less I knew the better. But it ... it was hot, and worth lots. Plenty for us to start a new life with."

"That was his plan. To steal a painting?"

She looked at Piers like he was an idiot, which be began to feel he was.

"Who was he stealing the painting from? Pierre Morel?"

She looked down and rubbed her hands together. "No. Morel was his boss. These were bad people. He said it would be best if I didn't know them."

"We need to know."

She shook her head then looked up at him. "I don't know."

"This isn't a game April. Who was he stealing it from?"

"I don't know! I told you, I don't know."

Sidney glowered at Piers. "She said she doesn't know."

"But if we're going to find this thing—"

"She's had a shock."

"I understand that, but we don't have long before those goons come after us again."

Sidney wrapped her arm around April's shoulder and stared hard at Piers. "You can still give her time."

Piers made a show of closing his mouth.

After a long silence, April stood up. "I have to go."

Piers looked up at her. "Where to?"

"I can't tell you."

He nodded. "I'm sorry about Auguste. I really am. And about ... just then."

Sidney stood and hugged the woman. "We're sorry. Really."

"You have somewhere to go?" Piers said.

She nodded. "Away from Paris. I have friends." She looked hard at each of them. "If you have any sense, you'll get out of Paris, too. These people are ruthless. Auguste said so. Trained killers. Some sort of army, special forces, people."

Piers nodded grimly.

Sidney rummaged in her pockets and held out a bundle of bills. "Auguste's."

April pushed them into her pocket and pulled out a handkerchief to wipe her nose. She didn't look at either of them. "They're bad people. Auguste wasn't a bad person. Not really. But they are. He said so. If you're innocent, go to the police. Quickly."

Without making eye contact, she pushed her way through the tables and chairs to the street, and disappeared in the crowds.

CHAPTER TWELVE

Piers led the way out of the café and scanned the road for Little and Large. "At least we shook them off."

Sidney sniffed for the umpteenth time. "I have got to wash."

Piers agreed. He stank. They wouldn't give anyone the slip smelling as they did.

She led them through intersections and office buildings until they reached the Seine.

"Are we going to jump in?" he said.

Sidney looked at him as if he had grown antlers. "Of course, you first."

"Okaaay, sorry."

"There's a shower station along here somewhere."

"Really?"

"No, I just made it up, for fun. What do you think?"

Piers looked at the dirty patches on the knees of his jeans. "You realize our clothes will still smell."

Sidney rolled her eyes. "Clothes will have to be next."

She turned left and threaded her way down a footpath to the road that ran alongside the river. A few minutes later they saw a squat, circular metallic building by the side of the road. A sign on the side bore a diagram of a water spraying from a shower head.

"Why do they have these things here?" said Piers.

"Why not?"

"But who walks around and suddenly decides they need a shower?"

"We need one."

"Okay, but we're an exception. How many people escape via a trash chute?"

"I've done it before."

"Escaped down a trash chute?"

"Needed a shower."

Piers laughed. "Bad date?"

"From hell."

He stopped laughing and followed her, not quite able to work out if she was serious. They arrived at the shower station. "It takes four euros," she said, her hand held out.

Piers sighed, rummaged in his pocket, and found four coins. She shoved them into a small slot and a metallic door slid back, revealing a tiny bathroom.

She stepped in. "I won't be long."

He grunted. The door clunked, a brake being released to allow the door to close. She forced a brief smile. The door started moving.

"It's four euros each," he said.

"Obviously." She rolled her eyes.

The door was halfway closed. He tapped his pockets, but nothing rattled. With a cry he threw himself into the gap. The door thumped against his chest, pinning his arms by his sides.

"What are you doing?" she said, trying to push him back out.

He shoved inward harder. "Stop it, stop it."

"I need a shower," she said.

"I need one, too."

"You can't be in here while I'm having a shower."

"I don't have any more coins."

"So? Get some."

"No! We need to keep a low profile, not advertise ourselves to every shopkeeper in Paris."

"And this is keeping a low profile?" she said.

The metallic door hissed and released the pressure for a moment, hoping to relieve the obstruction. He rotated his body and slipped into the cubicle as the door thumped closed behind him. He breathed a sigh of relief.

She punched him in the chest. "Now what, Einstein?"

He looked at the small space. The shower, sink, and toilet were made of a single continuous piece of plastic. The whole room could be washed down. There was a sign on the wall with instructions and a single mirror. He turned around. "I'll just look away."

She punched him in the back. "You better had."

He looked at her in the mirror.

"And not that way. Face the corner, away from the mirror."

He turned again. He could still see the mirror from the corner of his eye. She noticed him looking and slapped him over the head.

"Owww, sorry. I was just—"

"Just nothing."

She pulled off her jacket and threw it over his head. "You can hold my clothes."

He left the jacket on his head, and held his hands out. She piled her clothes into his arms. "Don't drop them."

"Wouldn't think of it."

"Better not. And no moving that jacket either."

He hummed his agreement.

The shower started and a fan above his head roared into life. The humidity rose and he was hot under her jacket. He flapped the edges to cool himself.

"You better not be thinking of shaking that jacket off."

"I'm hot."

"You're the one who pushed his way in here. Besides, you're going to have a shower in a minute, so stop complaining."

He heard water splashing and forced himself to think of anything but foaming lather draped over her smooth, wet skin. It didn't work.

"So, what are you doing in Paris?" she said.

"I had to update some software in a crane, but now I can't do it until Saturday. I thought I was going to be able to do some sightseeing."

"That sightseeing better not include me. You keep that jacket where it is."

"I am. I mean, I didn't, or wasn't, I—never mind. What about you?"

"Me, what?"

"What are you doing in Paris?"

"Long story. Where I lived things were getting worse. Then this guy got all mad with me."

"Imagine that."

Her voice raised an octave. "I know. Like, what's all that about? I try to get along with everyone. You've got to, right?"

His jaw froze up with his mouth half open. His mind raced through answers.

"Right?" she said, stretching out the word.

He nodded, trying not to make the jacket fall from his head. "Right, right. I mean, how could that happen?"

"Yeah, serves him right. Then, afterward, I find out he's married. His wife just about killed him."

Piers hummed his dubious agreement. "Yeah, certainly. Yeah. Serves him right. What was he thinking?"

"What about you? What's with your mummy problem?"

Piers screwed up his face. "What mummy problem!"

"Your mum. The woman on the phone. Sounds like she could be trouble."

"I don't have a mummy problem, and she's not trouble."

"Well, sounded like it. She didn't want to take no for an answer."

"She was worried."

"We were busy."

"I was hardly going to tell her I was too busy with a girl to talk to her, was I?"

"Could have."

"No, I couldn't." He put on a falsetto accent, "Hi mum, it's me, your son. I met this girl in a taxi while this guy died at our feet, and now a bunch of people are going to kill us if we don't find their painting. Have a nice day."

"Well, you don't have to be crazy about it. Surely, you can tell her you're talking to a girl without going all weird on her."

"I ..." He pursed his lips. She had a point. He breathed out. "I don't know."

"What do you mean you don't know? You have had a girlfriend before, haven't you?"

"W—"

"Oh, don't answer that. I'm done with sob stories for a while."

He huffed. "Yeah. This day hasn't exactly been much fun for some people."

"Tell me about it."

"I meant for Auguste. He got shot, remember?"

She clicked her tongue. "Yeah. Okay. Right ... April, too."

"I just wish she had told us more, like where he lived."

"You don't know?"

"No? You know?"

"It was on that paper."

"What paper?"

"In his wallet."

"I went through his wallet. It was just credit card receipts."

"There was a piece of paper, too."

"You've been keeping stuff from me?"

"No! We've been busy, in case you haven't noticed."

"For Christ's sake, you have to tell me everything if we're going to sort this out."

"I have to tell you everything."

"Yes."

"Right."

There was a long pause.

Piers sighed. "So, where's the piece of paper from his wallet?"

"In one of my pockets. You want to see it?"

"I'm stuck in a shower cubicle, holding your clothes with a jacket on my head."

"So, you want to check it later?"

He took a deep breath and exhaled slowly. "Yes."

"Okay, whatever you say."

He took another breath. And another. And another. "How much longer?"

"I've got to get clean."

He heard her hair slapping against her skin and swallowed. Foaming lather worked its way back into his imagination.

A couple of minutes later the shower stopped. "Don't take that jacket off."

"I won't," he said, slowly, hoping he masked his regret.

A hairdryer ran, blasting air through the cubicle. It was incredibly powerful for a hairdryer.

"Are there towels?" he said.

"No, you just dry yourself with this big blower thing."

He closed his eyes, hoping to block out the image of her body bathed in warm air. It didn't help.

After a few moments the dryer stopped. She rummaged in the pockets of her jacket without taking it off Piers' head, and pulled something out. He heard hair being combed until she said, "That'll have to do."

"Good. Can I take the jacket—"

"No!"

He felt her lift her clothes from his hands, one by one, then she pulled the jacket from his head.

She looked fabulous. Long curls coiled over her shoulders with devil-may-care abandon. Her cheeks were flushed, and her lips bright pink from the heat of the shower.

Her smile hit him full on. It broadened slowly, growing in intensity, spreading outward, lifting the corners of her mouth, pronouncing her dimples, framing the glint in her sparkling eyes. She patted him on the arm. “Thanks.”

He gulped before speaking. “Nits nar nata problem.”

“Huh?”

He gulped again. “Nits not a problem.”

She frowned. “Right.”

He stood awkward for a few moments.

“Well?” she said.

“Well what?”

“A shower. Are you going to have a shower?”

“Yes, right.” He turned to the shower. “Are you going to—”

“Look away? Ewww, yes. Of course.” She turned around to face the same corner as he had. “I’ve got my eyes closed.”

He removed his coat, decided not to ask her to place it over her head as she had done to him, and hung it on a peg on the wall. Then he took his shirt and jeans off and self-consciously folded his boxer shorts inside them. There was nowhere to put them.

“Would you hold my clothes?”

She held out her arms.

He flipped the lever that started the water. It was lukewarm. The soap was in a push button dispenser and he quickly covered himself in lather. He shivered. “Takes a while to warm up, doesn’t it.”

“You only get one shower for your euros.”

“Oh, thanks. Vital tip that.”

“You were the one that jumped in.”

He tried to keep his back to her. “This is getting bloody cold.”

“Hey, you have a scar.”

"I thought you had your eyes closed!"

"I can't stand here all this time with my eyes closed. It's not normal. How did you get your scar?"

"Fell out of a tree and tore up my shoulder when I was young."

"No, not the one on your shoulder. The one on your bu—"

He crunched up, covering himself. "Do you mind?"

"I was only trying to make conversation."

The water was freezing now. The overhead fan was still blasting away. He could feel his skin prickling with the cold. He swept a blob of shampoo through his hair and rinsed it away immediately, thrashing his hands to clear the soap off his body. He snapped the tap to off and ran his hands over his body to wipe off the water. "God, I'm cold."

"Turn on the dryer," she said.

He pressed the button and nothing. He pressed again. Then he thumped and banged it. Nothing happened. He was shivering uncontrollably. "Argh. One shower, one run of the dryer." He ran his hands over his body, trying to ward off the cold and flicking more water onto the sopping wet floor.

She leaned over to the sink and pulled a handful of paper towels from a dispenser. "Here."

"Are you closing your eyes at all?"

"Will you stop being a wimp?"

She juggled the towels in her hand and backward-passed them to him. At the same moment his clothes fell out of her other hand.

He dived to grab them from the wet floor. She did the same. Their heads cracked, his eye socket against the back of her skull. A storm of twinkling lights erupted in his vision and darkness threatened to overcome him. He slid down and sat on the floor. "Oh, god, why'd you do that?"

She picked up his clothes from the wet floor. "I didn't do it on purpose."

He grunted and held his head in his hands.

"Wow. You've got abs," she said.

He sighed. "Everyone's got abs."

"Yeah, but not ones you can see."

He drew his knees up to his chest. "That's because I've got no clothes on."

"I meant—"

There was an insistent knocking at the door followed by Little's high-pitched squeak. "You two are wasting time."

Piers rolled his head forward and groaned. The twinkling lights swam around in circles.

"Go away," said Sidney, "we're busy."

"So I can hear. You two lovebirds might be having fun, but you're wasting time. Get out here."

"Give me my clothes," said Piers. He heard a burst of schoolgirl sniggers from outside.

"Maybe it's just me, but he doesn't sound like a ruthless criminal."

"Don't forget the big guy."

"Maybe."

"And it's always the unlikely ones that get you into trouble."

She looked him up and down. "Tell me about it."

Piers opened his mouth, but she turned away and held out his clothes. He wiped himself down with the paper towels and wrestled on his clothes. They were wet, he was wet, and they refused to fit, but eventually he was clothed.

He looked in the mirror and flattened his hair. There was swelling around his eyebrow, he could see and feel it.

"What are you going to tell them?" said Sidney.

"Why me?"

"Oh come on, you're the best at talking to them. You know you are."

He looked at her and sighed.

She gave a bright smile and waved a scrap of paper. "I've got Auguste's address," she whispered.

Piers angled it toward him. "You know where this is?"

She nodded as she straightened his jacket. He stuffed the paper in his pocket and pressed the lever that opened the door.

Little and Large were stood outside. The small guy had a smug grin and he sniggered at the sight of them. “Finished, are we?”

“At least they’ve had a shower.” Large said, nudging Little.

Little screwed up his face. “And what’s that supposed to mean?”

“Well, you know, they’re clean.”

“You trying to say I’m not clean? I’m clean. I had a shower this morning.”

“Yeah, this morning, but not every morning.”

“Well, that’s just not ... oh, never mind.” The small guy scowled and turned back to Piers. “The boss wants his stuff back.”

“Stuff?”

“Yeah.”

“Exactly what *stuff* are we talking about?”

“Don’t get all intellectual with me. I don’t go for that sort of thing.”

Large gave a slow blink.

Piers said nothing and stared at Little.

The small guy shifted his weight from one leg to the other. “Well?”

“Well what?” Piers said. “If we don’t know what this stuff is, how can we give it back?”

“The boss thinks you were in on this. So you must know where it is.”

Piers sighed. “Is this *stuff* a painting?”

Little squared himself up. “Course it’s the painting.”

“And does this painting have anything to do with the shooting at Gare de l’Est?”

“Oh, whoa! We weren’t there. We didn’t have anything to do with that. Nothing. Understand?”

"So, the painting doesn't have anything to do with that shooting?"

"Well, I didn't say that. Just that we didn't have anything to do with what happened up there. Whatever it was. Which we really don't know about because we weren't there."

Large nudged Little with his elbow. "They get the idea."

Piers couldn't help himself. "Are you two trained killers?"

Little took a half step backward and puffed up his chest. "What kind of question is that? Do you really think I'm going to answer that? Would a trained killer really tell you?"

Large bumped Little on the shoulder. "I haven't been trained."

"What? A giant like you? You don't need training."

"So, you're not killers?" Piers said.

"Wait up, lover boy. Let's just say you don't want to risk anything breakable in my hands, if you know what I mean."

Piers blew out a long breath. "Oh yeah, I know what you mean."

Little gave a smug grin. "I'll bet you do. So, let's have some results before we have to do something very nasty with you, lover boy."

CHAPTER THIRTEEN

Rain forced Piers and Sidney to shelter under the awning of a small shop, but it washed the trash from the gutters, and to Piers' relief, many of the pedestrians from the streets. He adjusted his jeans. They were still damp from the shower. He pulled out the paper with Auguste's address. "How far is it to this place?"

Sidney shook her head. "We need to get clean clothes first, or has your nose stopped working?"

Piers shoulders sagged. "I know, but we're under a little pressure here. Can't clothes wait?"

Sidney glowered at him and sighed. "Damn you." She kicked at the ground. "All right. It's about a mile. But afterward, it's clothes."

"Okay. Excellent. We can walk."

"Haven't you noticed the wet stuff coming down?"

"I'm still wet from the shower. Besides, I am *not* taking another taxi."

Sidney adjusted her collar and prepared to step out into the rain.

"Oh, wait," said Piers, "the police might be there."

She gave him a glum look.

He thought the situation over for a moment. "Still, the police are everywhere."

"Right. So, we're going?"

"We could. Unless there's a lot of people about."

"So, you don't want to go?"

"Well, we might be recognized by a pedestrian. And there's the police. They're probably guarding his house and—"

"Do you want to bloody go or not?"

Piers stood with his mouth half open and his brow furrowed, staring at her. "Errrr."

She threw her hands up. "All right, we won't go."

He shook his head. "No, no. I think we should go. I don't want to, but we have to."

"Really? Because I don't want to rush you into anything."

"No, no, definitely, let's go."

Sidney readjusted her collar and they walked down a road lined with cafés. Striped awnings kept the patrons dry as they enjoyed their coffee. Piers watched as she passed nonchalantly through the tables and chairs, sweeping an umbrella from a man's chair before stepping back out onto the sidewalk.

Piers caught up with her as she popped the umbrella open. "What do you think you're doing?"

"Keeping dry."

"That was somebody's umbrella."

"Someone's" she said, stressing the *one*. "Somebody means some dead body, and I'm pretty sure dead bodies don't use umbrellas."

Piers scowled. "Even if they did, you'd nick it off them."

"I'll give it back," she said, shaking her head with her wide eyes staring at him.

"You don't think the guy might want it, like, now, when the rain's coming down? Or that he might call the police?"

"Oh, stop it." She moved to one side of the umbrella. "Share?"

Piers huffed "no," and carried on in the rain. After a moment, he slicked his wet hair back, muttered to himself, and moved under the umbrella.

She smiled at him. “Doesn’t that feel better?”

“It was—”

She held her finger over his mouth. “Da da da. No more complaining. I need to look after you. Especially if mummy isn’t around.”

“What’s that supposed to mean?”

“She obviously looks after you.”

“She does not!”

“Well, she didn’t sound very happy.”

“She wasn’t happy because this nutcase was wailing and crying right next to me. That’s not normal, Sidney.”

“I was trying to get us out of our little situation.”

“Little situation? We’re being followed by a pair of maybe, maybe not, trained killers who want us to return a painting we know squat about before them or their boss decide to do away with us, and you call that little?”

Sidney came to a stop at the end of a block, leaving Piers to walk on an extra pace, around the corner, out of the umbrella, and into the rain.

“What?” he said. “Does the truth hurt?”

“No.” She nodded across the street to a knot of police officers and yellow tape. “We’re here.”

Piers ducked back behind the corner of the building. “Why didn’t you tell me?”

“I just did.”

“I meant before I walked out into the full view of Paris’ finest.”

“I got us here, all right? I can’t think of everything.”

“What now?”

“How would I know? You were the one who wanted to come here.”

Piers groaned. He looked around the corner of the building. “We need a plan.”

"You're on fire today, aren't you?"

He rolled his eyes at her and looked up and down the street. "We need a distraction."

She gave him a sour look. "As long as it doesn't involve me taking my clothes off."

He screwed up his face. "Have I ever suggested—"

"I'm just saying."

He looked up and down the street. "There's a phone box over there."

"So?"

"You need to make a phone call."

She pulled out her mobile and waved it in front of him.

He shook his head again. "You need to phone the police. Give them a tip."

"Phone the police? Me?"

"Yes, you. Tell them you spotted the people on the TV a few blocks from here."

"Guy on the TV," she corrected. "They didn't have a picture of me."

"Okay, okay, tell them guy."

"And why do I have to call from a phone box?"

"Because they could track your phone to you, and then they'd know where you are and that you're involved."

"But phone boxes smell."

"I'm sorry. Try to stand outside."

"Men pee in them."

"Well, not this man. Maybe some men do, but this man doesn't."

"And women, too. I've seen that, you know. Women peeing in phone boxes."

"All right. Okay. Very sorry. Just make the phone call and get straight back here."

She stomped off, taking the umbrella. He watched her dance around the phone box, standing outside it, inserting her money, and holding the receiver with the tips of her fingers. She kept it at a distance from her mouth, spoke loudly, hung up, and walked back. "Done."

"Where did you tell them we'd been spotted?"

She pointed back the way they had come. "Down the street, turn left, then ten more blocks."

"What? So this is the quickest route?"

She nodded, "Yeah."

"Oh my god." He slapped his forehead. "We wanted to get rid of them, not bring them to us."

Around the corner shouts broke out among the police officers. With a squeal of tires, a string of police cars headed in their direction. Piers grabbed her hand, ready to run. She pulled him back, shoved him against the wall, and pressed herself hard against him. She popped open the umbrella and flipped it over her shoulder, blocking them from view, then pressed her face into his neck.

Piers heart thumped. "I—"

She shushed him and wrapped her leg around his, rubbing the back of her ankle up and down his leg. "Act natural. No Parisian will notice a couple kissing," she whispered, "but don't you dare let your hands wander."

"I—"

"Shut up. I know it's difficult, but act like you're enjoying it."

He folded his arms around her and stroked her back. Her breath was warm on his neck. He tilted his head to press his face to hers. He could feel the softness of her body pushing against him. She ran her hands over his shoulders and down his arms, squeezing his biceps playfully.

The tension in his limbs dissolved and a warm glow spread through him. A calm smile spread across his face. She rubbed her hand across his shoulders and her long hair brushed against his ear. He closed his eyes and squeezed her tight.

"You only have to act like you're enjoying it," she said.

He opened his eyes and loosened his hold. "I am," he cleared his throat, "acting."

"Good." She patted his back. Somehow he felt it wasn't part of the act.

A cavalcade of cars and motorbikes raced by, sirens blaring. He pulled the umbrella closer to make sure their faces were obscured. The sounds diminished and he risked looking out. "They're gone."

Sidney slid from him. He let his arms fall away slowly. He breathed out, stifling a sigh, and didn't breathe back in. Leaving her felt like a physical blow. It took all his willpower not to reach out for her. The rain had made her tousled curls a vague memory, but her eyes were bright and, even in the cold, her high cheekbones had a natural tint to them, the slightest of pinks, just enough to accentuate the flawless tone of her skin.

He watched, mesmerized, as she opened her mouth. "Now what?"

"Huh?"

"I said now what? I did my bit by phoning from the pee-box. What's next?"

He shook his head and took a gulp of cold air. The adrenaline and tension returned to his muscles. "Right, we have to go."

He turned the corner and headed toward where the throng of police had been. There were only a couple left on guard.

Sidney tugged at his sleeve. "Is this a good idea?"

Piers took her hand. "No. Start crying."

She looked at him.

"Start crying. Like before, on the steps. When we get there, just act like we're breaking up. Then come back over here and wait for me. Just don't give up easily."

She shrugged and started sniffing. Her tears built as they crossed the road and by the time they reached the guards she was balling her eyes out.

Piers shook himself free of Sidney's hand. "I've told you. It is not possible. We cannot continue like this."

She looked at him through eyes that were gaining bloodshot rings. "Why not?"

"My wife. Your husband. Not to mention the friends you bring to the parties. Non, non, it is all too much."

"So this is it?"

Piers bent his head down. "I am sorry, *ma chérie*." Then he turned, stepped to the police officer and tried to push past.

The officer didn't move. "This building has been secured, monsieur."

Piers look indignantly at the man. "Non, non. I live here."

Sidney grabbed Piers hand. "Please. You can't leave me. No one else uses leather like you."

Piers freed himself and re-addressed the officer. "Monsieur, really, I must go inside."

The officer shook his head.

Sidney grabbed Piers by the shoulders and pulled him a step backward. Piers wrestled himself free, colliding with the officer and pushing past.

"Sir, I—" said the officer, but Sidney crashed into him, her arms flailing.

The officer fought her back.

Piers paced backward into the entranceway of the building. "I have to go. We need to make a clean break of it. For her sake."

The officer struggled with Sidney. "No!" she called. "Don't leave me, don't leave me."

Piers stepped inside building, and headed straight up the stairs. On the first landing, he started checking the nameplates beside each apartment. On the fourth floor, he found he needn't have bothered. A door hung off its hinges and yellow crime scene tape had been draped across the entranceway.

He listened for movement before stepping over the tape. He found a bedroom, bathroom, and a small kitchen/living room with threadbare rugs over wooden floors. The furniture looked old, but well cared for. Pictures of April adorned the walls of the bedroom. In the entrance hall, a large color poster showed a panoramic view of a beach, busy with people. Piers guessed it to be in the south of France.

The living area had practically nothing in it. An old TV, a coffee table, and a paisley loveseat. Perhaps the police had already removed everything from the apartment?

From the window, he saw Sidney walking back to the corner where they had stood and hugged. No, he reminded himself with a deep sigh, where they had acted.

Only, he hadn't acted.

The feel of her body against his had been a shock at first, and her breath on his neck had been intoxicating. He'd had to tell himself to keep his hands on her back and nowhere else, but then she had embraced him, and the whole world seemed to go quiet. The cars, the trains, the voices—it was as if Paris had come to stop, holding its breath to see what would happen.

Only, nothing happened. They'd been acting. It had been a wonderful moment. A moment when she had washed away all his doubts. A moment when she had calmed all his fears. A moment he wished had never ended. But it had, and now he felt guilty standing in the dry apartment while she stood in the rain. At last she flipped open the umbrella. He fought back the urge to run downstairs and hold it for her.

He dragged himself away from the window. He was being stupid. She was beautiful, but a nightmare. And they'd only just met. It was infatuation. It would pass. Maybe.

He made for the kitchen. The cupboards were full of pots and pans, all well-used. He rummaged through them and found nothing. An enormous collection of sharp knives lined the work surfaces and Piers felt a chill as April's words 'trained killers' pushed into his mind.

He used a spoon to stir the sugar, the coffee beans, and the flour, but there was nothing hidden in any of them. The bread-basket contained an old French loaf, hard enough to be classed as an offensive weapon. Outside the kitchen window was a rusty fire escape that looked like it hadn't been used in years.

The bedroom was different from the other rooms. He felt uncomfortable as he looked at an array of candles and a line of furry animals. Auguste wouldn't have had them without April. Piers bit his lip as he remembered her walking off into the crowds. He should have treated her better. He hadn't appreciated Auguste and April's relationship, he'd only thought of him as the man that nearly got them killed, and her as a woman keeping secrets.

The scent from the candles was feminine and a blessed relief from the stink from his clothes. He gave a short laugh as he remembered Sidney's apartment. She dressed well, but her home had been a mess. Not dirty, just well-used. He ran his finger over the candles and wondered if there was a softer side of Sidney.

The closet was divided down the middle, April's clothes on the right, Auguste's on the left. Each of them had three pairs of well-worn shoes. He had a black umbrella in his corner, she had a red one in hers'. Piers looked back around the room. They had been very exact about everything. This man didn't improvise.

Piers drummed his fingers on the closet door. Auguste didn't just decide he was going to steal the painting on a whim. He'd planned it in advance—when he was going to steal it, how he was going to steal it, and how he was going to get away. It wasn't a heat of the moment thing. He had train tickets and his girlfriend waiting at the station.

The bathroom had April's touches, too. A painting of a sunflower hung beside the door and a line of creams and fragrances stretched along one side of the sink. Auguste's razors and shaving foam were in a cabinet above the toilet. The cabinet had a slope to it, and Piers had to catch a razor that fell out as he opened the door.

Under the sink there were the usual cleaning items and a metal bar with two points that Piers couldn't envisage a use for.

He slumped onto the edge of the bath. He'd found nothing. The place was a model for clean and organized. Everything had its place and everything was in it. April and Auguste shared the small space fifty-fifty, even-steven, right down the middle. He looked up with a wry grin, everything except the cabinet above the toilet, and who'd want to put anything in there, if it was going to roll out into the toilet?

Piers stood up and looked at the cabinet. The rest of the house was well looked after, organized, cared for. It wouldn't have taken much to adjust the cabinet so things didn't roll out. He ran his fingers around the edge of the cabinet. It was solidly fixed to the wall. He opened it up and saw why. The rear of the cabinet was metal and two tamper-proof security bolts secured it, top and bottom. He ran his finger over them. They were rough with small holes in them.

He heard voices downstairs.

He wrestled with the cabinet, but it wasn't going to move. Whoever put it on the wall, didn't want it to come off.

The voices grew excited, something about a hoax call, a misuse of police time, and tracing the call. The police were back.

He thumped the cabinet on the side. The razors and shaving foam fell out, clattering onto the floor and splashing in the toilet bowl. The security bolts were weird. They had a sloped surface with two small holes. French engineering, he thought, always got to be different. It'd need—

He dived for the cupboard under the sink and pulled out the metal bar. Its two points fit the bolt, and he rotated it as fast as he could. The remaining contents of the cabinet fell out, splashing toilet water down his jeans. He twisted on.

The voices were heading up the stairs. He heard calls for a fingerprinting kit and a photographer.

The first bolt fell out and he went for the second. The cabinet rocked on the wall and the bolt wobbled about. The lever slipped off, his hands slick with sweat. He reseated it and turned frantically. The cabinet sagged forward, obscuring his view of the bolt. He used his forearm to push the structure back onto the wall, but then he couldn't move the bolt properly.

He heard footsteps climbing the old wooden stairs.

He flipped the lever over to his right hand so he could hold the cabinet with his left, but lost hold of the lever. It crashed into the toilet bowl and clattered into the water.

The footsteps stopped.

His heart pounded against his ribs. He grabbed the cabinet and wrestled it back and forth, levering it away from the half-removed bolt. The wood splintered and cracked. He twisted the cabinet to one side. There was a compartment behind the cabinet with a small black plastic bag in the rear corner

The footsteps resumed, faster this time and accompanied by shouting.

He grabbed the bag and ran for the kitchen fire escape. The latches were stiff and dug into his fingers as he pried them open. The window creaked as he slid it up. He threw himself through the opening, not caring about the state of the rusty metalwork, and pulled the window down.

The steps were narrow and doubled back on themselves with each floor. He bounded down, two at a time, bending his knees to mute the sound. Only when he reached the second floor did he realize the bottom two floors of the stairs were missing.

He looked down. It was a long drop. Didn't the French have fire regulations? He cursed whoever had taken the last steps and considered hanging by his arms to get low enough to jump without breaking anything. He looked again. It would still be ten feet to the sidewalk.

He was beside a window. Inside was another kitchen. He kicked hard and the glass disintegrated around his foot. He stamped on the bigger of the jagged pieces that were left in the frame before squeezing through the gap.

His shoes crunched on broken glass. The apartment was identical to Auguste's, only the owner wasn't as fastidious about cleaning up. A dog stared at him from a basket in the corner. The room smelled worse than Piers. The dog wagged its tail and bounded over. Piers swept him up to keep his paws from the broken glass. The dog licked his face and Piers tried to wrestle him into a different position, one that kept his breath as far away as possible.

He ran for the door and dropped the animal onto the couch on the way. The dog bounded off the couch, and beat Piers to the front door, its lead in its mouth.

"No, stay here."

The dog bounced up and down.

Piers pushed the dog away and listened at the door. It was quiet. He clicked the lock and opened it an inch. There was no sign of anyone on the landing. Restraining the dog with his foot he stepped out. Before he had closed the door, the dog bolted past him and down the stairs. Piers gave chase, using his hands on the bannisters to leap five or six steps at a time. He reached the hallway at the bottom and his shoes slapped onto the marble floor. Two police officers at the door turned. The dog barked and dived between them.

"Stop him!" Piers said, shoving through the police officers and running flat out after the dog.

The dog went away from where he'd told Sidney to wait, but he didn't care. He ran after it, calling, "stop," and praying that it didn't.

After two blocks, the dog came to an abrupt halt by a gate into a park. He looked up at Piers, wagging his tail and shaking the leash in his teeth. Piers looked behind him and breathed a sigh of relief when he saw the officer hadn't followed.

He hooked the leash to the dog's collar. The dog wagged its tail, sweeping the ground in an arc behind him. The park wasn't big, but he couldn't simply tie the dog to a tree and hope he was found. His owner might not pass this way as they returned home, and he couldn't leave the guy there all night. Piers looked up and down the street, he couldn't walk the dog back to his home, either.

He toyed with the idea of handing the dog to the police outside Auguste's apartment, but that was still too much of a risk. The dog ran around his feet, wrapping him in the leash. He let go and untied himself. The dog looked up, and made small jumps while his tongue flapped from the side of his mouth.

Piers took a deep breath. The dog had gotten him out of trouble. The least he could do was look after him. They would walk around the block and get back to Sidney without passing the police in front of Auguste's apartment building. Then he would find something better to do with him.

Piers checked the name tag and rolled his eyes. Some people were so inventive. He patted the dog's head, and walked off to meet Sidney, Rover bouncing along beside him.

CHAPTER FOURTEEN

Sidney walked back to the corner and out of sight of the police officer. She wiped her eyes and blew her nose. This whole thing was ridiculous. Who knows what damage she was doing to herself with all the crying, running around, and falling down trash chutes. She ached all over, her eyes would be as puffy as could be, and the cold and the rain weren't helping. Even the brandy hadn't warmed her up.

She flipped open the umbrella. It had been a stupid trick to get by the officer, but it had worked. Though she wasn't quite sure what they would find out about the painting. Would Auguste have hidden it in his apartment? And if he had, surely the police would have found it already? In fact, what was Piers looking for? She furrowed her brow.

He was a weird guy. Likable. Kind of funny and kind of different. At least he wasn't full of lines and, she grinned, he could give as good as he got, like he wasn't just out to impress her. He had hung on to her longer than she'd expected when they hid from the police behind the umbrella, and she wasn't quite sure how much of his embrace had been acting and how much might have been a little more. There again, she smiled, that wasn't such a bad thing. It had been obvious in the shower that there wasn't an ounce of fat on him, and the feel of his arms around her had been—she licked her lips—nice.

A black Mercedes appeared at the end of the street. Its windows were dark and she felt uncomfortable as it passed by. It didn't look like a police car, but she couldn't shake the feeling she was being watched. The car turned right and raced away.

She looked up at the windows of the apartment block. Which one was Auguste's? And how long was Piers going to be? She felt strangely alone without him. She shook herself. No. She didn't need any man. Not again. She grinned. At least not for a while.

She heard a voice behind her. "Excuse me?"

Sidney's heart thumped so hard she could feel it in her throat. She whipped around, bringing the umbrella down as a shield. She gripped the shaft, ready to stab it forward into whoever had addressed her.

It took a moment for the face of the person who stood in front of her to register. He was tall and dark with square shoulders and a disarming smile filled with pearly white teeth. As she pointed the umbrella, he held his hands up in mock surrender. "Sorry, didn't mean to frighten you."

She swallowed. She didn't know what to say to the dictator who, for the past five years, had ruled her homeland with an iron fist and a ruthless secret police force.

He lowered his hands. "Please, put the umbrella down."

She lowered it a fraction. "What do you want?"

He smiled. "I know you have been in this country for a while, my dear, but surely you haven't forgotten me already."

She fought back a long list of disparaging names. "Per ... President ..."

He nodded and held out his hand. "Brunwald. Yes, my dear. And I must say I am very pleased to meet you."

She lowered the umbrella and shook Brunwald's hand. His grip was firm and confident. Her's was limp and cold as her muscles refused to cooperate.

"Don't worry. I understand why you had to, shall we say emigrate, to France. I sympathize with what you've had to go through. Our country was sick. It still is. We all must do what we can to achieve our dreams in life."

"He held his hands out, palms upward. "Your passion, I understand, is fashion. Mine, contrary to the popular opinion in the press, is to restore our beautiful country to health, to resurrect our pride, to cherish and protect the values we have held dear for millennia." He smiled.

Sidney forced her mouth closed and swallowed. "I, er, don't understand."

"I'm sorry, my dear, it is a lot to take in quickly. You see, I am here to personally retrieve various historical objects—those the criminal class have stolen from us. These people seek to undermine the progress we are making in Elbistonia." He clenched his fingers and shook them. "They wish to steal the very things that make us Elbistonians."

Sidney shook her head. "I ... I'm not ... I haven't stolen anything."

Brunwald smiled and patted her arm. "Oh, I am not accusing you. No, no, no. I know what you are going through to retrieve our art."

Sidney licked her lips. "Going through?"

"You do know the painting it is that you seek?"

She curled the ends of her lips downward.

Brunwald bobbed his head up and down. "Aaaaahhhh. I suspected as much. Not of you my dear, but your friend, I fear, has been a little less than fully truthful with you."

"My friend?"

"The convenient Mr. Chapman."

"Piers? Convenient?"

Brunwald nodded. "He has taken advantage of your kind and generous Elbistonian nature."

"He has?"

Brunwald nodded sagely. "Indeed he has. Have you wondered why you two met?"

She shook her head.

"He was already in the taxi when you got in, correct?"

She nodded.

"Have you wondered why?"

"He was closer to the taxi than me."

The sympathetic smiled returned to Brunwald's face. "No, my dear. He was waiting for the other man. For Auguste. The man who stole the painting. They were in this affair together."

Sidney's cheeks fell. "He was?"

Brunwald nodded. "At the railway station? Don't you find it was curious he was able to identify Auguste's companion so quickly?"

"She had a phone."

He gave a sympathetic smile. "Even so. A trained professional would struggle to find an unknown person so quickly. And the apartment over there. You brought him to this address, but did he ask for the apartment number?"

Her eyes narrowed their focus.

"You see, my dear, he has been using you. Playing you along."

"But he—"

Brunwald leaned forward. "No, my dear. He is using you as cover and will dispense with you soon as he has what he wants. If you really don't believe me, consider what happened in the taxi."

She thought for a moment. "I got in. He was already there. He refused to get out—"

"Uh-huh."

"Then Auguste got in. Then the shooting started and we drove away."

"Did Auguste say anything?"

"No."

Brunwald straightened up. "Nothing?"

Sidney pinched her lip between her teeth. "Well ... wait ..."

Brunwald leaned closer. "Yes?"

"He did say something about Waterloo. Piers works for Waterloo. And he spat at him."

"Auguste spat at Piers?"

"Yes."

Brunwald furrowed his brow. "I see. He must have known he wasn't going to make it, and was venting his anger at his brother in crime."

Sidney looked into Brunwald's eyes. "Do you think?"

Brunwald's face remained impassive and he nodded slowly, deliberately, exaggeratedly.

Sidney slapped her hand over her mouth. "Oh my god."

"Don't blame yourself, my dear. His sort use and abuse everyone they come in contact with. You haven't done wrong. Quite the contrary. You are perfectly placed to do your country a great service."

"I am?"

"Indeed. As I said, I am engaged in rounding up the many pieces of art that have been stolen from our country. You may have heard about it. Our government is, of course, trying to manage the situation and the adverse publicity, but we must recover what is ours, do you not think?"

"Yes, but—"

"What can you do?" Brunwald smiled. "That's easy, my dear." He pressed a slip of paper into her hand. "My personal number. Text me. Keep me updated of what you find. No detail is too small. The people involved. Their locations. Oh, and there is money involved. Knowing who has it would be just as important as retrieving the painting."

Sidney bit her lip. "Right. Ummm ... "

"You are concerned, my dear, I understand."

"Er, no. I was just wondering, what is the painting?"

Brunwald gripped her elbow. "You don't know? It is The Angel. *The Angel of the Cross*."

She gasped and her eyes narrowed. "From the Basilica?"

Brunwald held his index finger over his mouth. "It is something we are most keen to keep quiet, my dear. Can you imagine the hurt and anguish that would be caused by the news of this theft, if it were to be confirmed? And all for some lowlife's tawdry desire for mere money? No, no. This is something I wish to recover at all costs." He gripped Sidney's hands. "Something you and I must do, if we are ever to make our country right again, my dear."

A horn sounded. Sidney noticed the black Mercedes was parked just yards away.

"I must go now. Please do not fail me. With your help, we will rebuild our great country. Once again, we will able to hold our heads high in the world. We will be proud of our history and our achievements."

He gave her hand, the one holding his phone number, a squeeze, and bowed his head. "Goodbye for now, my fellow Elbistonian." In a moment, he was in the Mercedes and the car was purring away.

She stood numb as she watched the small plume of vapor from the car's exhaust trail around the corner and out of sight.

Boucher Brunwald! Boucher Brunwald had talked to her. To her. The man who'd used the army to take control of Elbistonia when the riots had started. The man who had installed himself in the old king's palace. She swallowed. The man who had a brutal reputation. People called him Brunwald the Butcher with good reason. Though not within earshot of his secret police. She'd even fled the country because things had become so bad.

But perhaps things hadn't all been his fault? Riots and political unrest had been tearing the country apart until he took control. He had been ruthless, but perhaps he'd had to be? Maybe it had been criminal gangs that stirred up the unrest?

Besides, he was here in Paris to find *The Angel.* The painting had hung in the Basilica for five hundred years, the single greatest symbol of their country. He was here to take it back. From criminals. Him. Personally.

She looked at the phone number. She might have fled the

country, but *The Angel* was going to be returned to the Basilica if she had anything to do with it.

She pulled her phone out. As she entered his number into the address book, she heard her name, half called, half hissed. She looked up. Piers stood in an alleyway across the street, staring at her.

Her skin prickled. How long had he been standing there? Had he seen her with Brunwald? Had he heard their conversation? There was only one way to find out.

She rammed the paper into her pocket, and smiled with all her might.

CHAPTER FIFTEEN

Piers waved Sidney to cross the road and join him.

A frown spread across her face as her eyes locked onto Rover. "What have you got there?"

"A dog."

"A dog?"

"Yes, it's a dog, all right. D-O-G. Dog. Man's best friend and all that. He got me out of trouble, but now we're stuck with him."

"Whoa. You're stuck with him. I'm not even sure I want to be stuck with you."

"Thanks very much."

"No offense, the dog's probably fine, but I've got this whole finding-the-painting-and-not-dying thing going on."

"And I haven't? I went in that bloody building. Walked in through a bunch of police and escaped out the back when Inspector Clouseau returned, all on the off chance of finding a clue to a painting that might keep us alive."

"With a dog."

"Yes, with a dog." Rover paced circles around Piers. "He helped me get out without getting caught. We can't walk him back home. So, we'll just hang on to him for a while and take him back when all this has quieted down."

"You mean when we've found the painting."

Rover circled Piers. "Yes, okay. When we've found the painting. What's gotten into you? You're suddenly all serious about finding the painting."

"That's how we sort this mess out, isn't it?"

Piers untangled the leash from his legs. "Yeah."

Sidney wrapped her arm through his free arm and they started walking. "So, what did you find?"

Piers took a deep breath. "The place was very tidy and neat."

"And?"

"They shared the space. Very organized."

"So that was it? That whole visit to his apartment and all you know is they were clean, tidy, and each visit comes with a free dog." She wrinkled her nose. "And a smelly one, at that."

"Leave the dog out of this."

"I wish I could. This is serious, Piers."

"All right. I know, I know."

"And we stink."

"We can blame it on the dog."

She glowered at him and stomped off.

"Wait! Where are you going?"

"I'm going to get new clothes. I am not going to smell worse than a dog."

Piers pulled the black plastic bag out of his pocket and chased after her, waving it in the air. "Wait, wait. I found this."

She stopped and grabbed the bag out of his hand. "And when were you going to tell me?"

"I just did!"

"I asked you what you found and all you told me was how clean the place was."

"You asked what I found."

"Exactly."

"I found the place clean."

"Do you really think I was interested in that?"

"Well—"

"Perhaps I should have asked about the color of their drapes."

"Give it a rest."

"Pah!" She flapped the bag in his face. "And what else did you find, eh?"

Piers stepped back. "Nothing. That was it. The place was empty apart from that."

She gave an exasperated sigh. "Sure."

"Really," he said.

Rover hopped over and rubbed against her leg. She pushed him away.

"Really," he repeated.

Rover moved gingerly back and stood beside her.

"Well, I guess we'll find out one way or another." She tucked the bag inside her jacket and walked off. "I'm still getting new clothes."

CHAPTER SIXTEEN

Piers ran after Sidney. "We can't just go shopping. We need to check out that bag."

"We? So you're including me in your plans now, are you?"

"When haven't I included you?"

"How would I know if I wasn't included?"

He screwed his face up. "I don't understand. Look, we need to find somewhere quiet to open the bag."

She glowered at him. "Quiet? What's the point?" She pulled out the bag, dug her fingernails in and ripped it apart.

Piers glimpsed a flash of something shiny, and caught it. "It's a key." He turned it over. "There's a number."

He tried to look in the remains of the bag. She moved it away from him, pulled out several sheets of paper, and flipped through them. "Swiss Free Bank. Safety deposit box." She turned the page over and gestured for the key. He handed it over and she compared the key and the papers. "Different numbers. We're screwed."

He held his hands out. "Can I?"

She glowered at him before handing the papers over. He looked through them. "What's the number on the key?"

"It's no good. There's more digits in the account number."

He raised his eyebrows. "Please?"

She grunted and read out the key's six digits.

He smiled.

She snatched the papers from him. "What?" Her eyes bored into him. "What?"

He forced himself to stop smiling. "The key's six digits are in the middle of his account number."

She furrowed her brow and flipped from examining the paper to the key and back again. "What do you know?" She smiled. "You're not just a pretty face."

He couldn't help himself grinning. She drove him mad, she defied all reason, and she changed her moods faster than Parisians drove, but she was the most wonderful person he had ever met, and he trusted her completely.

CHAPTER SEVENTEEN

Sidney stuffed the key and papers into her pocket, and set off fast.

Piers raced to keep up, Rover only too pleased to bound alongside. "Will you stop?"

"Why? You got another admission to make?" She continued her rapid walk.

"No, I don't know where we're going."

"I do."

"Well, I don't and we need to—"

"Need to what? Work as a team? The same sort of team that kept the existence of the black bag to himself?"

"I didn't keep it to myself. And you have the bag."

She huffed. "And how can I trust anything you say?"

Rover and Piers kept up, trying to stay alongside her. They walked along a line of shops until Piers called for them to stop.

She stood with her hands on her hips. "What?"

He pointed to the shop behind her. A bank of TVs displayed the frozen image of a girl, one eye half-open and the other closed, rushing toward a Métro exit. Her mouth was wide open and her tongue stuck out. Her wet black hair formed clumps that zigzagged across her head. Her jacket was twisted sideways and the roof-mounted camera was pointed down the cleavage of her blouse.

Sidney groaned and slapped her forehead.

He turned and she was already stomping off down the street. He gave chase. "Okay, so they have a picture of you, but it was a miracle they didn't get a picture on the motorbike."

"Oh yeah, right. They couldn't get a picture of me on the bike, could they? No. No action shot for me. No dramatic pose. No catching my best side. No, no, no. For me it's the five-franc hooker look. The bimbo who's been groped by every drunk at the bar."

"What are you talking about? It's not that bad. Besides, it might slow them up identifying you."

"Great consolation. I look like a tramp and that might slow up my identification. Yeah, great, thanks."

"I meant—"

"I know what you meant. You meant you're all right and you don't care about anyone else."

He grabbed her hand, dragging her to a stop. "Stop it. This is stupid. It's a picture. It's a bad picture, yes, but it's just a picture."

She shook him off. "Just what you'd expect a man to say."

"It's the truth."

"Pah!" She resumed walking.

He breathed deep and followed her. Rover trotted dutifully, his head down, concentrating on his steps.

She turned down an alley and a minute later, just as Piers thought they had doubled back they emerged into Place des Vosges.

He touched her arm. "Is the Swiss Free Bank around here?"

She gave an exaggerated sigh. "Do you use your eyes at all?"

It took only one glance. "Sidney. We need to find this bank, not go shopping."

"What bank is going to talk to us in these stinking clothes." She punctuated each syllable by poking him in the chest. He grabbed her hand, but she pulled away and walked off.

He followed her past the cafés and boutiques that lined the arched walkway around the buildings. Fluffy pastries nestled between elegant china, and mannequins displayed haute couture. Nowhere did he see a price tag.

He felt for his wallet. He daren't use a credit card. The police had his picture, and maybe his name, so they would track them in moments. "We can't buy anything here. I don't have enough cash."

She looked at him. "I wasn't expecting you to buy me anything."

"Okay, I was just thinking, we can't use a credit card."

"Listen, do you want a change of clothes or not?"

"Okaaay."

She walked on past a long string of designer boutiques until she came to one with an alley down the side. "This one."

Piers looked in through the window and saw rustic wood floors with occasional items of clothing hung from statues, and what seemed to be real miniature trees. The clothes in the window were a uniform bright red. A giant lava lamp bubbled in the corner, and sequins were sprinkled over the floor. He glanced at his bargain basement jeans. It was just his sort of place.

He tied Rover to a bench under the shelter of the arches. The dog sat with his tongue out, and watched them go.

Sidney gripped the door handle. "Just do as I say, understand?"

He raised his eyebrows. "Okay."

They went inside, and she tucked the umbrella into a stand behind the door.

A stick-thin girl appeared from behind a giant mushroom. She wore a fluorescent blue oriental-patterned dress, a glitter-covered black beret, and flat black shoes. Her nose wrinkled as they approached.

"Bonjour," she chimed in a singsong voice.

"Bonjour." Sidney's thousand-watt smile burst out and her voice went up an octave. She explained they were looking for new clothes after they had had an impromptu dip in a fountain. The girl took the idea in her stride, looked Piers over and, to his surprise, quoted his size correctly.

"And you will be swimming again?" she said.

"I don't think so."

She looked dubious. "Shoes?"

He looked at his bedraggled Marks and Spencer specials. "Uh-huh."

The girl departed, leaving Piers standing and Sidney looking over the items hanging from the trees. He couldn't help but notice that one of the outfits she looked at seemed uncannily like the one she was wearing. He stared hard and Sidney saw him. She gave him a cold stare and placed one finger over her lips to silence him.

The girl came back with several suits, all very slim and in a shiny fabric. He chose a dark gray one with a fine pinstripe. The girl didn't ask about a shirt but simply handed him a bright white one and a thin black tie. He took them to a small, enclosed area with a revolving mirror for a door.

Outside, he could hear Sidney and the girl discussing the merits of various dress, suit, and shoe combinations. He was glad to catch Sidney steer the conversation away from the red items in the window. Red didn't have a molecule of low profile to it.

To his surprise, the outfit was his size, though the jacket was cut for a tight fit. He looked at himself in the mirror and got the immediate impression he had turned into an extra for the set of *Mad Men*. At least he didn't smell like a dumpster anymore.

The girl knocked on the mirror and handed him two pairs of shoes, both extremely pointed. He chose the one he thought would inflict the least long-term damage and thanked her. She gave a smile that was at least 900 watts lower in intensity than Sidney's.

He emerged, standing straight and looking sharp. The girl

was suitably impressed. Rover stared through the window with wide eyes, but Sidney paid him no attention. She took several patterned dresses into the changing cubicle and closed the rotating mirror.

The girl fussed over Piers' suit. "It makes you feel happy, no?" said the girl.

Piers kept a straight face. "I guess."

She walked around him. "We could take it in a little."

"No, no. Its fine."

"Just don't get it wet." She wagged a finger at him. "No swimming."

"I'll try not to."

The girl nodded approvingly.

A phone rang. His phone. The sound rattled from the changing room. Damn, he hadn't emptied his pockets into the new outfit. Without warning his old clothes came flying over the top of the cubicle's walls and clattered on the ground. His phone stopped ringing. He retrieved it from his pockets just as it rang again.

"It'll be mummy," Sidney called.

He looked at the display and flipped it open with a sigh. "Hello, mum."

The girl turned away. He was sure he saw a smile creep across her face.

"Piers. You never called me back, dear. I waited and waited and you know I was worried but you didn't call back."

"I've been busy."

"I know, dear, you said before. Very busy. Has that girl stopped crying?"

"Yes, mum. She's stopped crying."

"Well, I certainly hope you weren't upsetting her."

"No, mum, I wasn't upsetting her—"

"Because it sounded like it."

"I wasn't upsetting her."

Sidney spoke from the changing cubicle. "Not then, he wasn't."

"Mum, I wasn't upsetting her."

"I know, dear, you said."

"Yes, I did."

"Is this a girl you know?"

"Sort of, I guess."

"You don't sound very sure, considering she was crying over you."

"She wasn't crying over me, mum."

"Are we going to get to meet her, dear?"

"No, mum, no. No, I doubt it. She's ..."

"She's what dear?"

"Ummm, she's ... she's—"

"Oh, Piers! Don't tell me she's pregnant!"

"No! She is not pregnant. Definitely. Nothing like that."

"Don't lie to me, Piers."

"Mum. She is not pregnant."

The girl behind the sales counter quickly averted her gaze and busied herself with her paperwork when she noticed Piers looking in her direction.

"Well, this is a turn up. You go abroad and meet a girl who is crying to you and who isn't pregnant."

"She is not pregnant. And you meet people, you know, and things happen."

"Things? What things, dear?"

"Nothing, mum. There's nothing to worry about. The girl's not pregnant, I'm okay and there's nothing for you to worry about."

"So you said, but mothers worry about these things. Not that I'd expect you to understand a woman."

"I do understand women."

A bark of laughter erupted from the changing cubicle along with several indecipherable mutterings.

"I have to go. My, er ... taxi's here. I have to go."

"A taxi? Where are you going?"

"Have to go, mum. Call you later."

He mashed the off button with a sigh of relief.

The girl behind the counter was still busy with her papers, studiously avoiding eye contact.

The rotating mirror spun, and Sidney walked out of the changing cubicle. She wore a tailored floral dress with a medium neckline and short hemline. The material shimmered and bounced as she walked, propelled by every touch of her curves.

She rotated back and forth, admiring herself in the mirror, twirling the skirt, fascinated with the way it moved. Her smile evaporated the moment she saw Piers was just as fascinated.

"This'll do," she said.

"It's wonderful," Piers said.

She grunted. "Well at least you told her I wasn't pregnant."

"Oh, what, my mum?"

"Unless you've told anyone else that I'm not pregnant lately?"

"No. She was just worried. The previous call. The crying. The, you know, everything."

"Everything? Everything such as there's a fictitious taxi waiting for us? Or that you're okay?"

"It's complicated."

"Everything with you is."

"No, not everything is complicated. Just some things."

"Like the truth."

"No. It's just ... to protect her ... she'd worry."

"Course she's bloody worried, you're lying to her all the time."

"I'm not ... Not all the time. Just things she wouldn't understand, like being abroad."

"She can't be frightened because you're in Paris?" She spread her hands out to gesture to the city. "I mean, is the War of the Roses still going on?"

"The War of the Roses was in England. It was the Hundred Years War between Britain and France."

"Oh right, that helps clarify everything, doesn't it?"

She turned away from him and faced the girl. "I'm going to need a coat. Wool. Something durable." Sidney cast a disparaging glance at Piers, "You better get him... something similar."

The girl disappeared behind a multicolored series of overlapping circles and emerged with two coats. Black. Matching.

"Twee," Piers said.

"No," said the girl, a shocked look on her face, "Ralph Lauren."

They both tried them on. Piers' was too tight. He handed it back. Sidney took hers off. "I'd better have a larger size, too."

The girl looked puzzled. "But it seemed to fit perfectly, madame."

Sidney shook her head. "I'm going to need something with a bit more room to move. Life's been action-packed since he turned up."

The girl smiled.

Sidney shook her head and frowned. "Sadly, it's not what you might think. So far today I've been shot at, rescued on a motorbike, threatened by the mob—"

Piers' face fell. "Sidney, stop it."

"Forced down a garbage chute—"

"Sidney." Piers grabbed her elbow.

"Showered in a public cubicle," she shook him off, "forced to lie—"

"Sidney."

"And gained a dog."

The girl's eyes went wide. The features of her face seemed to move in slow motion. "Oh. My. God." Her hand flew to her face and she started bouncing up and down on the balls of her feet. "Oh my god, oh my god, oh my god."

Piers touched Sidney on the arm "I think we need to go."

"No!" said the girl. She rushed around and stared at Piers' face from different angles. "My god. You're the man on the motorbike, the guy on TV. I should have known. Everyone's talking about you. That was soooo brave."

"Brave?" said Sidney, her face screwed up.

"Oui, how he rescued you? C'est magnifique!"

"You obviously don't know him like I do."

The girl clutched Sidney's arm. "You are so lucky."

"I'm lucky to even be alive after meeting him."

The girl shook her head in awe. "In the middle of such danger, he whisks you away. Ahhhh."

Piers looked at Sidney with a smile that she didn't return.

"Okay. We need to go," Piers said.

The girl's eyes widened even further. "Oh non, non, wait, wait." She pulled out a phone from behind her counter. "I need a picture. Pleeeaaase."

"This might be exciting news for you, but we're trying to keep a low profile."

The girl waved her hands. "I know, I know. Now you are being hunted by the police. It's like, like, like Bonnie and Clyde. It is so romantic."

Piers stared at her. "Bonny and Clyde ended up dead."

The girl shrugged and regained her composure. "Please, you must let me have a photograph."

"Well."

Sidney put her arm through Piers'. She gave her best smile and hugged him toward her. He joined her smile and the girl took a picture. She waved her phone in front of Sidney who oohed at the photo.

"Just one more," said the girl, "please?"

She took several more, moving them around the small shop, snapping away.

"We've really got to go," said Piers.

Sidney flipped through the pictures on the phone while the girl added up the bill.

"Can we have a talk," whispered Sidney, dragging him into

the cubicle. She took a deep breath. "This isn't working out as I planned."

"Meaning?"

"Well, she's nice."

"And?"

"Nice. She's nice. She's so excited to see us, and she took pictures ... of us. So, we can't, I mean, I can't, maybe you can, but I can't..."

"What? Can't what?"

Sidney leaned in close. "Run out on her."

"Run out on her? In these clothes? Was that your plan coming here? Try a few things on and steal them?"

Sidney crossed her eyebrows. "All right. We're not all blessed with a sugar mummy."

"I don't have a sugar mummy."

"She's phoned you three times in one day. I'd say she's looking after you."

"She just doesn't have anything else to do."

"Except look after you."

"All right, all right. So, if your master plan of stealing these things isn't on, what now? I don't have enough cash, and I'm guessing you don't either since I've paid for everything since we met."

"Oh, right, money. Just like a man."

"Look, I'm just trying to be practical."

"Oh, yeah, the dog catcher. You're all about practical."

"What's that supposed ... oh, never mind."

She stared at him and he stared back. He cracked first. "I have to pay with a credit card, don't I?"

She gave a sheepish smile. "She's been so nice. Took pictures and everything."

"Pictures? Is that all you think of?"

"Pictures are important."

"What's important is that the police will have our location the moment she swipes my card."

"Maybe not."

There was a knock on the mirror door. Piers flipped it open.

The girl was outside. "I couldn't help overhearing. Sorry." She shrugged. "I know you don't want me to swipe your card, and I totally don't want to be the one who gets you caught. So, I was thinking, maybe I could write down the number and I'll charge it later."

"Really?" Sidney grabbed hold of the girl's hands. "That would be great. Really great. Wouldn't it, Piers?"

The girl beamed.

"Oh yeah ... great," Piers said.

Sidney and the girl stared at him. He blew out a deep breath and gave a smile. "I'm sorry. Yes, that would be great. Its been a stressful day. We're making this up as we go."

The girl's smile returned.

Piers pulled out his credit card. She wrote down the number. "I'll charge it tomorrow, okay?"

"That should be enough," said Sidney as she looped her arm through Piers', "Because, apparently, I'll be traveling by taxi with a man who understands women."

The girl sniggered, but Piers was frozen to the spot. Beyond the miniature trees, the red outfits, and Rover's big eyes, police officers were spilling into the grace and tranquility of Place des Vosges.

CHAPTER EIGHTEEN

The girl pushed Piers and Sidney through racks of clothes. "Out the back. There's an alley. Vite, vite. I'll lock the front door."

"Rover," Piers said.

"Leave the dog," Sidney said.

"We'll have to come back—"

The shop assistant kept pushing. "I'll look after him. Go!"

Piers didn't need any more encouragement. He flew through a small stockroom and hit a fire escape door at full speed. It crashed open and he piled into a narrow lane. Sidney ran past him, tugging at his arm. He took off after her, his new shoes slipping on the old, wet flagstones. Sidney looked back and waved her arm, urging him on. She took another alleyway that emerged onto a main road.

He followed her to the right and into a Métro station. She stopped beside a ticket machine but his wet leather soles didn't, and he slipped, sprawling all over the floor, taking out several people in the process. He struggled to his feet, apologizing profusely as a cluster of weary travelers swore at him.

Sidney moved around the back of the throng and pulled him out of the growing mass of unhappy people. "Come on. Forget the tickets. We can get out on the other side of the station." She led them through a maze of tunnels and up a flight of stairs, back to street level.

Piers kept grabbing at the leash that wasn't there. "You think Rover will be okay?"

"That was the best name you could come up with?"

"It was on his collar."

Sidney squeezed his arm. It felt good. She smiled at him. His heart skipped and he felt a wave of heat rush over him. He knew his face would be red. He looked away.

She shook his arm. "He'll be okay. That girl will look after him."

"Right."

"We need to look after ourselves."

"Yeah." He patted her hand on his arm.

"There wasn't anything else in Auguste's apartment, was there?"

He looked at her quizzically. "No, why?"

"Nothing. Just, you know, you've been under a lot of stress." She wrapped her arms around him. Her hair brushed over her face and he could smell her skin. She went from one extreme to another. He hesitated to hug her back.

He felt her hands pat his back. "I'm sorry. I've been hard on you. We need to work together as a team, right?"

He slowly closed his arm around her shoulder. "Course."

She ran her hands down his sides and up and down his arms. He swallowed. The tension melted from him. It felt wonderful to feel her touch. He tightened his hug and relaxed his head onto her shoulder.

Her hands slid over his waist and hips and he felt his phone bump against his side. After a few moments she patted him one last time and took a step backward, separating them.

Piers felt the chill air where her warmth had been. He wanted to reach out and pull her back, but her smile had faded.

She stared at him. "So there was definitely nothing else at Auguste's?"

"No. I told you. Nothing else."

She turned. "Okay, then. Let's try the bank."

"Wait a minute." Piers stuffed his hands in his pockets, almost expecting his phone to be gone. "Were you searching me?"

"No!"

"You were frisking me!"

"I was not."

"You were checking me over."

"I was not!"

"I'm not hiding anything from you, if that's what you think."

"I was not frisking you! I was ... it was just a hug, okay? Next time I won't bother."

She stomped off and he followed.

Ten minutes later they arrived at the Swiss Free Bank. It was a bland modern building with windows all along the front and a revolving door in the center.

Inside, he could see potted plants, light wood furniture, and a row of tellers that looked busy. To one side, several desks with signs for bank loans, mortgages, and other services were lined up. "Other services" sounded like the person he needed. He held his hand out. "Give me the key."

She stared at him. "Why?"

"You need to stay here while I go in."

"No. I don't want you forgetting something again."

"I'm not going to forget something. I didn't forget the bag at Auguste's place, I'd only just escaped from the police and had a few things on my mind."

"Right. So, this time I'll go with you and we won't forget anything."

"If we go in together and anyone's seen the TV were going to stick out like a sore thumb."

Her eyes glazed over for a moment before snapping back onto him. "Okay. I'll go. On my own."

Piers sighed. "You?"

"What? You think I can't do it because I'm a girl?"

"No, no—"

"Then what? Why can't I do it? Why do you have to do it?"

"Because the key fits Auguste Chevalier's safety deposit box. He's a guy."

"Was."

"Right."

She nodded slowly and held up the key. He reached out, but she wrapped her fingers back around it. "What if they have a picture?"

"Picture?"

"Of Auguste."

Piers lowered his hand. "You mean I won't match the picture."

She smiled. "That's decided then. I'll go."

He nodded. "Okay. Might be better. Anyway, there's a lot of research that shows people are more cooperative with beautiful people."

Her thin eyebrows inched slightly closer together. "You mean that?"

"Course. I read it in Scientific Ameri—"

"No, stupid. Do you really think I'm beautiful?"

"Oh." He opened and closed his mouth, then swallowed hard. "Do we have to do this now?"

She stared, waiting.

He rolled his eyes. "Yes... of course. Yes. Beautiful. Gorgeous. Stunning."

"Really?"

"People practically line up to gaze at you."

"But what do you think?"

He could feel every thump of his beating heart. He licked his lips and lowered his gaze. "I ... well ... you're ... all of that and more."

"Really?"

He nodded. "I wouldn't have said it if I didn't mean it."

She gave a reluctant smile and mumbled something.

He leaned forward. "Huh?"

"I said thanks... and ... you're kind of ... okay, too."

Piers laughed. "I've always wanted to be kind of okay."

She punched him with both hands. "Okay, well, now you are. So stop complaining."

"I wasn't complaining."

"Good, because ..." She looked at the bank. "Let's just get this over with."

Piers took out his phone and they exchanged numbers. He watched as she finished typing. "What are you going to say in there?"

"That I want to get into the safety deposit box."

"And when they ask why you're not Auguste Chevalier, or at least a male? What then?"

She rolled her eyes. "This is France. No one will think anything of a man having a female assistant." She tossed her head back and flipped her hair over her ear. "Especially if they're gorgeous." She took a deep breath. "Wish me luck."

"Yeah." He touched her arm. "If you get worried, call, and I'll see what I can do."

She smiled and placed her hand high on his chest. "My motorbike hero going to come to my rescue again?"

He bit his lip. "Don't draw attention to yourself. And don't stay long."

She took her hand slowly off his chest, nodded, and walked off to the revolving door. He sighed, wishing he'd found something else to say, just to prolong their closeness.

He angled the umbrella to hide himself from the road and looked into the bank. He saw her approach the "other services" desk and sit down opposite a young man.

Minutes went by. Piers shuffled from one foot to the other, unable to see what she was doing. He felt a vibration in his pocket and pulled out Auguste's phone. "Swiss Free Bank" glowed on the display. He flipped it open. "Bonjour."

A young male voice at the other end addressed him. "Monsieur. Pierre Rockeutfort at the Swiss Free Bank. I was wondering—"

"Ah. My assistant has arrived?"

"Er, yes, monsieur. She is asking for access to your safety deposit box. She says you need to replace your records?"

"Yes, I know. We ... need to replace our records."

"I see. This is a most unusual request, monsieur."

"Maybe, but I still need to replace my records."

"Perhaps you could confirm your assistant's story."

"What story?"

"Of what happened to your records?"

"Right." Piers own phone buzzed. A text message from Sidney. He struggled to open it up as he talked. "What happened to the records? Right. Well. There was er, a—" He read Sidney's text message aloud. "Flood."

The young man continued. "That is what your assistant said. But I'm curious about how a flood could have happened on the fourth floor."

"Ahhhhh, yes. Curious. Yes, yes, indeed. I would be too. Right. Yes. A flood. Well ... the flood happened as a result of a ... fire. Yes, a fire."

His phone buzzed with another text message that read "Break-in."

"I see, monsieur," said the young man, "That's not quite the story you assistant told me."

"Right, right, yes. That's because that's not the end of the story, you see."

"Monsieur?"

"The flood was caused by a fire that was caused by a ... break-in. Yes, yes. The criminals broke in and started a fire, and putting the fire out caused the flood."

"I see, monsieur."

"Yes, I know. It's a long story. That's why I was hesitant to tell it. Remarkable really."

“It is, monsieur, but it does agree with your assistant’s story. We do like to check these things for security.”

“Good, now if you don’t mind I’d like my assistant back as soon as possible. There is a lot of … er … tidying to do.”

“I understand. I will send her back as soon as possible.”

“Thank you.”

Piers switched off the phone and stared through the bank’s windows. The young man opposite Sidney was busy at a keyboard. After a long minute, he beckoned Sidney to follow, and they disappeared through a doorway into the back offices of the bank.

Piers breathed a sigh of relief. People only had safety deposit boxes if they had something important to keep. He had a good feeling they were going to find something. The feeling lasted until he saw a police car converging on the bank and screeching to a halt in front of its revolving door. Piers’ heart thumped into his mouth.

Officers leapt from the car before it had even come to a halt. One man stayed in the driver’s seat while the others piled through the revolving door, one-by-one.

Piers paced toward the entrance. What the hell could he do? Sidney was out of sight somewhere inside the bank. They must have recognized her. He bit his lip. The phone call had probably been a ruse to play for time.

He pulled out his phone and dialed Sidney. She answered on the fifth ring, just as he thought it would go to voicemail.

“Sidney, the police are here. Get out now. Use a different route.”

She didn’t say a word, but he heard the click as she mashed the off button on her phone. Piers stamped his foot and swore. Were they holding her already?

Through the windows, he saw a bank official quickly lead the police to the door Sidney had used.

With the umbrella in front of him, Piers walked to the police car. He saw Sidney return to the lobby through a different door.

She looked around and started for the exit. Piers' heart thumped. She looked too uncomfortable, too suspicious.

He breathed hard. What the hell could he do?

He reached the bank entrance. The police car was directly outside with its engine running. Sidney was almost at the revolving door.

He rapped on the police car's glass. The driver cracked the window open. Piers stood so his face was above where the man could see, and pointed into the bank. "Quickly. The Inspector's in trouble."

The man twisted to look up at him. "Huh?"

"The Inspector asked for you."

The man popped open the door.

"Vite, vite." Piers pointed to the bank door while keeping his back to the driver.

The driver seemed uncertain.

"He sent me to get you," said Piers. "Vite, vite."

The driver jumped from the car and barreled through the revolving door.

Piers slipped into the police car's driving seat and put the car in reverse as Sidney exited the revolving door.

He saw the police running back into the lobby followed by the young bank clerk clutching his groin. Piers floored the accelerator. The car rocketed backward, bounced wildly as it mounted the curb, and smashed into the revolving door, wedging it solid.

He leapt from the driver's seat and raced past Sidney, grabbing her hand and dragging her down the street. He didn't look back and she didn't need any urging. They ran flat out, with Sidney shouting directions. After a couple of minutes, they slowed. She led them through a department store and out of a side exit. She bent over, clutching her side. Piers was panting hard.

"Damn," she said.

"You have a way with words."

She massaged her stomach. "That hurts."

"Sorry," said Piers.

"You bloody well should be. Next time you steal a car, let's use it to get away, huh?" Her eyebrows were at angles as sharp as her tone.

"It was all I could think of at the time."

The angles on her face melted and she gave a snort of laughter. "It was pretty funny."

Piers smiled. "I can't wait to see that on TV."

Sidney waved two envelopes. "I can't wait to see what's in these."

CHAPTER NINETEEN

Piers' feet ached. After running from the bank, they had settled into a steady walking pace, and he'd lost track of how far they had traveled. "Sidney, we've got to stop and think."

She came to a halt and Piers almost walked into her. "You think we're far enough away?" she said.

"Much farther and we'll have to swim the channel."

"More coffee?"

He shook his head. "I've had enough caffeine to keep me awake for weeks."

She held her hand out as if to sample the weather and looked up into darkening clouds. "Which we're probably going to have to do."

He furrowed his brow.

She rolled her eyes. "Stay awake. We're not exactly going to check into a hotel tonight, are we?"

He clapped a hand on her shoulder. "That's brilliant."

She brushed him off. "If you're trying to be funny, it's not working."

"No. A hotel. We don't need to get a hotel. I've already got one."

"You own a hotel?"

"No! I have a room booked in the company's name, not mine. They always do that. Corporate policy."

"Er."

"It'll be all right. We can hide out, think, and sleep."

"Together?"

"Yes. I mean, no. No, no, I don't want to sleep with you. I just meant—"

"You don't like me?" She gave an angelic smile, angled her head, and blinked at him.

"No, I do like you."

She fluttered her eyelashes. "But you don't want to sleep with me?"

"Exactly. No, I mean, I didn't mean it like that."

"What? I'm not your sort?"

"No. I mean—"

"So, what is your sort? What sort do you like? Let me know and I'll see what I can do to set you up with your sort."

Piers fell silent. She wrapped her arm around his shoulder and squeezed. "Why do you take everything so seriously?"

"Our lives are at stake, in case you'd forgotten."

"I haven't forgotten, but I have another idea."

He cocked one eyebrow.

She winked, "Since you're not keen on the idea of sleeping together."

He shrugged. "Very funny. We need a plan. It's not like we can stay awake at an all-night rave."

"Oh." She looked sheepish.

"You were thinking of going to a rave?"

"No! A club." She dug two tickets from a pocket and handed them to Piers. "It's just off the river. Bernard's. I know the owner. They stay open all night."

He turned the tickets over in his hands. "It's hardly a place to sit and think."

"I wasn't going to sit and think. It's Friday night."

"It's Friday night and we've got the mob and the police after us. Great time for a dance."

"What do you do on a Friday night?"

"I, er, I meet up. You know. With friends."

"Friends?"

"Yeah, I have friends."

"Female friends?"

"I have male friends and female friends."

"Right. Right. Clubbing?"

"Well ... maybe ... sometimes."

"What do you do on the other times?"

He straightened his back. "You know. Meet up. Have a few drinks. Go out and have a laugh."

"Tell me about the females you know."

"Well, there's lots. I mean ... well, my boss is a woman."

"Your boss?" Sidney slid her arm off Piers. "What do you really do on a Friday night?"

Piers opened his mouth, but she placed a finger across his lips. "No. What do you really do?"

He sagged back down. "Sometimes I meet up with a couple of friends of mine. We go for a beer, or play Xbox."

"Grand Theft?"

"Huh?"

"You play *Grand Theft Auto*, don't you?"

Piers looked down at his hands. "Okay. So I don't have much of a life compared to you."

"Nah, I played it once. Crashed a lot. You just need to get out a bit more. Meet some real people. Relax."

"You mean go to this club?"

She shrugged her shoulders. "I know people there."

"But—"

She wrapped her arm around his and pulled them close. "They have good music. We could dance. Have fun. You and me."

Piers' skin prickled and he licked his lips. His heart banged in his chest and he forced himself to relax his hands. He stared, brow furrowed, not breathing, with his mouth half open.

"Come on." She pulled playfully on his arm and winked. "Promise I won't leave with anyone else."

He pulled back. "Leave with anyone else? Dancing? People? Fun? Have you forgotten the fact we're on France's most wanted list?"

She hung on to his sleeve. "No! Besides, you don't know that."

"Know what?"

"That we're on the most wanted list."

"We've made a good effort to get there."

She let go of him, slumped onto a low wall and sighed. "So what's your plan?"

He took a deep breath. "I think the hotel is best. We need to look at the stuff you got from the bank."

She surveyed the street and pulled out two envelopes. "Let's just look at them here."

Piers spun around, looking for Little and Large, or the police.

She pulled him down onto the wall. "Will you stop doing your best to look suspicious?"

He sighed.

She opened the first envelope and pulled out one sheet of heavy paper. "His will," she said despondently.

Piers looked it over. It only filled half a page. "He left everything to April."

Sidney pulled a sheaf of papers from the second envelope. They were layered sheets of thin pink, yellow, and tan paper, glued along one edge. She sighed and handed it to Piers. "Sales receipt for a car."

He looked down the sheet. "A Renault LE, with optional side stripe and FM radio. Purchased fifteen years ago."

"Great," she said. "This doesn't tell us anything."

"It's the car April mentioned. She called it the old car he worked on every weekend."

"It is pretty old for a car. Even older in Paris."

Piers flipped through the pages. They were all carbon copies. He saw nothing suspicious, nothing that might be a coded message or a clue. "Bugger."

"You British. Such a way with words."

"What do you expect? We don't have a clue to anything."

"You think I don't know that? Have you forgotten I was the one who walked into the bank to get that? Or that I was the one running out when the police arrived?"

"I—"

"Forget it." Sidney snatched the papers from Piers and they sat in an uncomfortable silence.

"Don't you know anything else about Auguste?" she said.

"Like what?"

"Anything?"

"I don't know him any more than you do."

"Right."

"I don't. I never met the guy, and you know as much about him as me."

"You were in his apartment."

"So? I told you. It was tidy and practically empty."

"And you knew which floor it was on."

"Huh?"

"You knew which apartment was his. Among all the others you could have picked, you knew which one was his."

"You think I knew him? I never met the guy before."

There was a long silence.

"Besides, the door to his apartment had been kicked in. There was yellow police tape across the entrance. You couldn't miss his apartment."

She looked sideways at him. "Really?"

"Really."

"Oh."

The silence returned.

A Fiat 500 parked across the street from them and flashed its lights. Piers squinted to see inside. "Great. Little and Large have returned."

Sidney looked down the street. "There's a place down there we could eat, get out of their sights. Looks run down. I doubt they'll have a TV."

They walked to the restaurant. She was right. The place looked as if it had been swept when the Second World War ended and never cleaned since. The chalkboard outside had an illegible scrawl where the meals should have been written. Sidney didn't even stop to look, she walked straight in and sat down.

Piers gave up trying to interpret the chalkboard and joined her. "So, what do we do now?"

"Eat."

"Very funny."

She ordered an omelet and Piers a steak. Any meal might be his last, so he thought he might as well enjoy it. They sat in silence until the food arrived.

Piers took one look at his meal and knew it might actually be his last, it was almost entirely pink. "I can't eat this."

The waiter looked at him.

"English," said Sidney.

The waiter grunted and scooped the plate away.

Piers threw up his hands. "Great, so now I don't even get to eat?"

"Don't be ridiculous. He's going to cook it some more."

Sidney ate her food with a tiny fork. She was delicate, taking small portions and eating slowly. Even so, she was finished by the time the waiter returned with his steak.

The waiter dropped the plate on the table. "English," he said and walked away without waiting for a reply.

Piers tapped the steak with his knife. It wasn't just well-done, it was almost toasted. He cut off a chunk and chewed. To his surprise it tasted good, even though it gave his jaw a workout. He swallowed. "So, what do we know?"

Sidney stared at him. "Know?"

"About Auguste. About the painting. About what we're going to do next."

Sidney looked away. "You're the one who thinks he knows everything."

"When did I say that?"

"You told your mother, or have you forgotten already?"

He grunted.

Sidney stared at him. "Do you remember anything he said in the taxi?"

He shrugged. "Not exactly. There was a lot of shooting going on."

"Come on, think. He must have said something."

"He mentioned the company I work for."

"Which is kind of suspicious."

"Suspicious?"

"Yeah." She leaned forward, her brow furrowed. "You sure you didn't know him?"

He glowered back. "Positive."

She stood up.

"I haven't finished," Piers said.

"I'm going to the restroom."

She picked up her phone and walked off down a long corridor. Piers watched her go. He didn't have a clue how much the dress had cost, but the view from behind alone made it worth every penny. He pushed another chunk of steak in his mouth and looked around the café, only to realize he wasn't the only person who noticed her leave her seat. The other male patrons brought their gazes back to their tables and made themselves busy as he stared at them. He cut off another chunk of steak and stabbed it with his fork. Who did they think they were?

He chewed his steak and wondered the same question about himself. Without the taxi, the shooting, and the mob, he wouldn't have dared talk to her, and he doubted she would have given him the time of day. He swallowed, and shoved his gloom to the back of his mind. He had to concentrate on the problem.

And that was the problem. They had no clues. One minute they were arguing over a taxi, the next the mob was after them for a painting the dead guy had apparently stolen. Piers chewed another piece of steak. Auguste didn't have the painting in the taxi, so he must have hidden it somewhere. An obvious conclusion, but of no practical help.

He took a satisfying crunch of fries and almost forgave the waiter his attitude.

Sidney walked back, smiled, and dropped her phone onto the table. Piers watched her all the way.

She waved a hand in front of his face. "You don't have to keep staring at my figure."

"I'm not."

"Gee, thanks. You're just a bundle of compliments."

"I'm thinking about Auguste."

She hummed. "Is he your sort?"

"This is important. He jumped in our taxi at Notre Dame, right? But the other shooting happened at Gare de l'Est."

She nodded slowly.

"And we think they're connected."

She continued to nod.

"So how did he get between the two?"

She shrugged. "Taxi? Métro? He was out of breath and sweating. Maybe he ran?"

"Yeah. Only he was an organization freak. His house looked like it was out of a museum, compared to yours."

"Thanks."

"Then he has his will made out and stored in a bank. He's Mr. Prepared, yet he ends up chased across Paris like a madman with a painting he planned to steal."

"And your point is?"

"Planned to steal. He was a perfectionist. If he intended to steal the painting, he would have had it all planned out. He would have had an escape route, he wouldn't be jumping into a taxi."

"So? He messed up. It happens to the best of people, you know."

Piers shook his head. "No. He planned to get to the Montparnasse railway station in time to meet his girlfriend. But it's a long way. He'd never have done it on foot. He had a plan, I'm sure of it."

"Look, you're very irritating sometimes. What? Why? How does this help?"

Piers took a last bite of his steak and put down his knife and fork. "Things didn't go to plan. That's why he ended up running across Paris and jumping into a taxi. "

Sidney leaned forward. "So what? How does that help?"

"Get a map."

She straightened herself up. "What?"

"Get a map, a street map."

"What do you think I am? A walking map vendor strolling Paris on the off chance of making a sale to a demented Brit?"

"Fine." He grabbed a free tourist map from a tired looking display and spread it on the table. "Auguste starts off here, at Gare de l'Est." He drew his finger across the map, "and ends here, at Notre Dame."

"About two miles."

"Right. And somewhere along this route he dumped the painting."

"You're really narrowing it down."

"Let's just keep thinking."

"But he could have gone in thousands of different ways. There's so many streets."

"Do you think he was a good runner?"

"That man? If he hadn't been shot he probably would have had a heart attack."

"So, he ended up on foot not far from Notre Dame."

Sidney leaned forward. "And?"

"And he certainly didn't plan to use a taxi or the Métro to escape."

"Maybe."

Piers leaned back. "If he was going to escape, he'd use a car. The—"

"Renault."

"Exactly." He smiled. "All we have to do is find his car, and we find the painting."

"Damn. You really are pretty good at this thinking thing. Even if you are, you know, a bit annoying about it."

"And once we have the painting, we'll be free."

He grinned, excused himself and headed for the restroom. As he left, he noticed she was typing on her phone, and the café's males were paying her attention again. He had to fight back the urge to tell them to look somewhere else, but he was being stupid. There wasn't any romance between them, they were just two people stuck in a bad situation. One of them just happened to be devastatingly beautiful.

When he returned to the table, she smiled. It was close to her full thousand-watt version, but he couldn't help but think it was tinged with something else.

Auguste's phone rang. Sidney looked at the display. "It's them."

She flipped her phone open and smiled. Not the thousand-watt version, something altogether different. Something filled with boundless confidence—a confidence that bubbled over into her voice. "Yep."

Piers could hear the short guy's high-pitched voice rasping out of the back of the phone. "If you've stopped for lunch, I take it you've found the stuff."

"You're a bundle of laughs," said Sidney.

"More laughs than our boss will be, that's for sure, missy. You need to get your act together. Spend less time eating and more time finding our stuff."

"Stuff, stuff, stuff. It's probably not your stuff anyway."

"Who says?"

"Piers."

Piers rolled his eyes.

"Ohhhhh. Lover boy."

He leaned forward and spoke into the phone, "I'm not her lover boy."

Sidney turned away from him. "You can say that again. He doesn't even like my figure." She winked at Piers.

Piers flushed hot and leaned back in his seat. "I didn't say that."

"He sounds like a very sensitive guy," said the little man.

"Believe me, he is."

"Don't forget, you've only got 16 hours left."

"Until what?"

"Until you run out of time."

"I'll be biting my nails then."

"Ho-ho. Very clever. Think I'm simple, huh?"

Sidney hummed for a moment. "Tell your boss we don't have the stuff and we can't find it. Have a nice day."

She clicked off the phone.

Piers shot forward. "Bloody hell!"

She looked indignant. "What?"

"Have you forgotten their threat? And that they're a good deal bigger than either of us."

"The little one isn't."

"It's not the little one I'm worried about. Ring them back now. Tell them it was a joke."

"No."

"What? They're outside. They'll just wait for us to walk outside and beat the daylights out of us."

"But we know where the painting is. We'll be in control. They'll have to do what we want, and we'll be free. You said so."

Piers groaned. "Maybe. When we have the painting. It may have escaped your attention, but we don't actually have the painting yet."

Sidney's face fell. Her lips curled down and her eyes seemed to get smaller. "Then what do you want to do?"

"Call them back. Say you're sorry."

As she glowered at him, Auguste's phone rang. She flipped it open without looking.

"What?"

"You need to take this seriously. Our boss isn't a nice guy. Well, I didn't mean that, he is a nice guy, but sometimes he's not, *comprende?*"

"*Comprende?* My, you are well-educated."

"Well I am, as it happens. Very. Now, find our painting, and pronto."

"*Comprende* and pronto, all in one phone call. How lucky can a girl get?"

"Find the bloody painting."

The phone clicked off.

Piers shook his head. "They found us again. They might be idiots, but don't antagonize them, because they might be idiots with guns and knives."

"They don't look like they could handle guns."

"You'd be surprised. Especially if you push them over the edge."

"I'd be only too happy to push them over the edge."

He smiled. "I'd be only too happy to get rid of them as well, but for the time being we have to put up with them."

"Maybe we should take the knives, for safety."

Piers looked at his knife and laughed. "You'd be better off with the fork than this knife."

She wiped her fork on her napkin and slipped it into her handbag.

He rolled his eyes. "Is there anything you haven't tried to nick?"

She pulled a face at him.

He took a last mouthful of fries and pushed the plate away. The waiter arrived, scooped it away and dropped the check, all without speaking.

Piers glanced at the amount and dropped a couple of bills on the table.

"What now?" said Sidney.

He finished his coffee. "We start at Gare de l'Est and follow the route Auguste took. Which means we've got a long walk."

She stood up and headed for the exit. "No, it doesn't. Come on."

CHAPTER TWENTY

Piers chased Sidney out to the sidewalk. Little and Large were parked across the street. Little grinned at him from the driver's seat and tapped his watch.

"Come on," Sidney said as she stepped out into a small gap in the traffic.

Little's grin disappeared in an instant.

"Wait!" Piers leapt out into the road and grabbed her arm. "What are you doing?"

She shook him off. "If they're going to follow us around then they can give us a lift."

"Are you mad? We want to get away from them, not closer."

A horn honked and they jumped back onto their side of the street.

"It's a long walk." She shrugged, "What have we got to lose?"

"Them. We want to lose them."

"Come on, you can handle them."

He heard the Fiat's engine rev and the gears crunch.

Sidney ran across the road and stood in front of the car, her hand on the hood. "Wait, you can drive us."

Little waved *no*.

Piers dodged the traffic and reached Sidney. "We can't do this. This isn't good."

"Stand there," she said, pointing to the front of the car.

Little waved at him to get out of the way.

Sidney opened the passenger door. Piers held his breath. If Large punched her, she'd really be hurting. To his surprise, Large got out of the car and folded himself into the rear.

"Get lost!" said Little. "You can't get in here."

Sidney waved to Piers. "Come on, get in."

Piers looked at Large and the space beside him. "There's no way I'll fit in there."

Sidney ducked down and flipped open the canvas roof. "Go for it. I need to be in front to give directions."

Little reached to close the roof. "Leave that alone."

Sidney slapped his wrist and he drew his hand back.

Piers squeezed into the tiny rear space.

Large looked at him. "Sorry. Weren't expecting passengers."

"No problem. This is fine. Thanks."

Sidney slid gracefully into the front seat.

Little stared at her. "What do you think you're doing? We're trained killers you know."

The big guy leaned forward and spoke in a hushed tone. "Give it a rest. We just do cars—like this."

Piers put his hand to his forehead. "You stole this car?"

Large looked sheepish. "If I had known we were going to have company, I would have got something bigger."

"We need to get out," said Piers.

"The best thing you've said so far, lover boy," said Little.

"Gare de l'Est," said Sidney. "And we're not getting out, you are driving us there. Or Piers here will sort you out."

"Sort us out?" said Little.

"Sort them out?" said Piers.

Large rotated his shoulders then smacked his first into the palm of his other hand. "You wouldn't want to do that now would you?"

"No," said Piers. "No, I wouldn't."

"Oh, yes he would," said Sidney. "He's the worst of the worst and you don't want to get on his wrong side. Gare de l'Est, now."

"And why would we drive you there?"

"Because we'll get out there. Because we might find your *stuff*, and because," she jerked her head toward Piers, "he might hurt you if you don't."

Little gave Piers an incredulous look.

Sidney ignored him, sat back in her seat and buckled her belt. "Come on, vite, vite."

Little muttered, shoved the car into gear and lurched out into the traffic.

Large grabbed the driver's seat and leaned forward. "Would it be better if I drove?"

"It's a light clutch," said Little. "It's grabby. It's small cars. I'm not used to them. I usually drive sports cars and stuff."

"Oh, yeah, right. You should have said. I could have nicked a Ferrari instead, Reynard."

Little screwed his head down into his neck. "Don't say my name."

Large winked, "Sorry. And that may or may not be his name."

"Riiight," said Piers. "Thinking of secrets, how do you two keep turning up everywhere we go?"

Large nodded toward Piers chest. "You've got Auguste's phone."

"You're tracking it?"

Large pulled out an iPhone. "There's an app for that." He smiled and nodded toward Piers' clothes. "Plus, you're not exactly hard to spot."

Piers' face fell. "Riiight."

They drove on in a silence that Piers was very grateful for. The air blowing over his head from the open top was refreshing while he was squeezed in the tiny rear seat. The sights and sounds of Paris passed by, mainly honking horns and pedestrians shouting at passing cars. The smells went by, too. Mainly diesel and urine. Sometimes it seemed like there wasn't a single piece of Paris that someone hadn't peed on.

Little broke the silence. "What are you going to this place for?"

"A walk," said Sidney.

"You better not be planning to leave Paris. And I mean it."

"We're going for a walk."

"Why?"

"None of your business," said Sidney. "Just drop us off on the corner and you two can get a late lunch."

"We're not going to get lunch. We're going to watch you two."

"We could," Large said, "I'm famished."

"How can you think of eating at a time like this?"

"A time like what? It's almost—"

"Stop!" said Sidney, thumping her hand on the dashboard.

Little jumped on the brakes and dived for the curb, ending up parked at an angle, poking out into the traffic. "What the hell?"

Sidney unbuckled her belt. "We're close enough." In a moment she was out of the car and holding the door open for Piers. He ignored it and pushed himself over the folding roof and out the rear of the car.

A delivery van behind them honked its horn.

She slammed the door and leaned over the open roof. "Right. You two go and enjoy your meal, and we'll see what we can find."

"Oh, no. We're going to stay here, watching you."

The delivery van honked longer.

Sidney tapped the side of the car. "Better get a move on. You're blocking the road. See you in an hour."

She walked off and the Fiat crept out into the traffic. As it went by, Large put his hand up to wave. Little yanked his arm back down.

CHAPTER TWENTY-ONE

Piers and Sidney stood side by side. He could see the square in front of Gare de l'Est. A television van was parked in one corner, and police were clearing up the yellow tape and paraphernalia of a crime scene.

"Not that way," he said.

"Really?" she said. "Your brilliance amazes me."

He pulled out the tourist map and folded it to get Gare de l'Est and Notre Dame visible at the same time.

Sidney looked over his shoulder. "Where did he come from before he jumped in our taxi?"

"I didn't have time to ask. I was too busy having an argument with this other person who jumped in my," he looked at her sideways, "*our* taxi."

She punched him in the ribs. "I saw it before you. It was my taxi."

"Oh, right, the old Paris taxi etiquette. I forgot."

She smiled. "You know I made that up, right?"

Piers gave a mock look of shock. "You're kidding."

"No. That ... I—"

Piers beamed. She dug her knuckles into his side. Her face lit up as she laughed. He wrestled her hands away. "I really don't know what to make of you."

"Ditto," she said, squeezing his hands. "But we need to find this painting."

"Right." He took a deep breath. "Auguste must have approached the taxi from behind, otherwise we'd have seen him running toward us."

She pointed to the map. "If he was driving, the best route would be along Strasbourg, Pont Au Change, Saint Michael, then a right turn over to Montparnasse station. Easy. If the traffic's not bad, which it always is. So he'd probably use the side roads."

He looked along the route. "That's a lot of roads."

"What color was the car?" Sidney said.

Piers flipped through the sales receipt. "Blue."

She grabbed the paper. "Is that all it says, blue?"

She studied it for a moment and shoved it back into Piers' hands. "Must have been written by a man."

They set off along the street. Within a minute, Piers spotted a blue Renault LE. He ran to it. It looked old, but in good condition. There was no stripe, but it could have worn off. He cupped his hands around his face to look in through the windows. Empty fast food wrappers were everywhere and the ashtray was full.

"Can I help you?" said a voice behind him.

Piers spun around. "I'm, er, we're looking for a friend's Renault."

A well-dressed man sneered at Piers. "Really. Well, this isn't it. Get lost."

"We are looking—" Piers said.

Sidney dragged him away by the elbow. "Don't make a scene."

Piers freed himself from Sidney's grip. "Scene? You're a good one to say that."

The man got into the Renault and pulled out to a chorus of car horns. Piers watched the car disappear in the traffic.

Sidney shook him back to the real world. "We need to find the painting. We have to focus now."

"Wow. Suddenly, you're all business."

"What's that supposed to mean? I thought you were the one who wanted to take this more seriously."

"I do."

"Then get walking and start looking."

Piers took a deep breath and let his nerves calm. She was right. One minute he was the one focused on the painting, the next it was her.

For the next two hours, they walked along the alleys and side streets checking an endless string of blue cars until Sidney called a stop and leaned against a railing. She pried off one shoe and massaged her foot. "This is stupid. Like trying to find a needle in a haystack."

Piers stretched the backs of his legs. "Next time, let's kick Little and Large out, and we'll keep the car."

"You've waited all this time to think of that?"

Her phone buzzed. She read a message, pressed a couple of buttons, and stuffed it back in her pocket. "Friend. Doesn't matter. Come on."

"Where?"

"To walk this bloody route."

Piers sighed and followed after her. He rearranged the folds in the map to keep up with their location. Thirty minutes later, the Seine came into view. "That's it. I've had enough," she said, stopping on the sidewalk.

"There's only one more street," Piers said.

She looked at the last side road before the bridge to the island on which Notre Dame sat. She shook her head. "Sometimes I hate you. Lead on."

A cardboard *No Way Out* sign had been shoddily tied to a lamppost at the street's entrance. Sidney glanced down the road. "A dumpster, a dead end, and no sign of a Renault." She sighed. "Any other bright ideas?"

Piers folded the map. "There's a few more roads on the island."

"They can wait. I'm going to sit down." She walked off for a café. Piers took one last look down the dead end. "Wait."

She stopped and looked back at him. "I need to sit down."

"No. Look. Waterloo Large Construction."

She rolled her eyes. "So?"

"That's my company."

"Terrific. I'm going to sit down."

"Auguste spat at me when he saw the logo on my shirt."

She threw her hands up. "Maybe he didn't like your cranes spoiling the view. Maybe your company turned him down for a job. Maybe," she shook her head, "maybe he just didn't like you."

"Or, maybe he hated Waterloo for a reason."

"Didn't you hear what I said?"

"Wait a moment." Piers started down the dead end. The road was blocked off a hundred yards down from the entrance. Cars lined either side, some of them double-parked to make the most of the dead end. The yellow dumpster had seen better days. It was the large sort. Piers forgot how much it contained, but he knew the big cranes were used to lift them onto 18-wheelers.

As he walked toward the dumpster he saw something else, a small patch of dirty color poking out behind it. He quickened his pace. It was hard to tell, but as he saw more of the color he started to run. Seconds later he was staring at a faded blue Renault LE. The stripe along the sides was missing from the passenger door. Probably as a result of accident damage and a re-spray. He waved to Sidney. She trudged toward him.

He walked around the car. It was wedged in by the dumpster. There were several holes in the tailgate that were large enough he could poke his middle finger into them. Through the windows he could see the holes lined up with holes in the seat backs.

He heard footsteps, which turned into a run. Sidney grabbed his arm. "Is this it?"

He nodded. “There are bullet holes in the rear.”

Sidney bounced up and down with her hands clasped together. “Yes, yes, yes!”

He took hold of her hands. “Calm down. Don’t forget, we don’t want to attract attention.”

She breathed out then stooped to look in through the driver’s side window. “Is this definitely it?”

Piers tried the door. It opened with a creak. He looked inside before sliding into the seat. The glove box was empty as were the door bins, but wedged under the passenger’s seat he found a four-foot-long tube.

“Is that it?” Sidney said.

He looked up, unaware she had pushed her head into the car.

The tube opened easily, and the contents slid out when he shook it.

“It’s a painting,” Sidney said.

Piers folded over a portion of obviously fragile fabric. “Certainly seems to be.”

“Is it the right one?”

“How would I know?”

“What’s on it?”

He held it up so she could see. The head and wings of an angel were visible, with what looked like storm clouds and a rising sun behind.

Sidney gasped and grabbed hold of the door for support. “My god. That’s it.”

Piers slid the painting back into the tube. “You all right?”

She swallowed and looked at him. “Of course. Why shouldn’t I be?” She reached out to take the tube. “We just found the painting. A famous painting.”

Piers moved the tube away from her. “You know it?”

She ducked back out of the car. “Well, you know, I kind of recognize it. I couldn’t tell you what it’s called or anything.”

“But you said *that’s it*.”

“What is this, the Spanish Inquisition?”

"No. But I didn't know what painting we were looking for."

"So what? You think I knew?"

"Apparently."

She screwed up her face. "That's rubbish. It's a painting. I vaguely recognize it and I'm sure it's valuable. That's all."

Piers levered himself out of the car.

Sidney grabbed him by the shoulders and shook him. "We figured it out. Well, you figured it out, really. But we found it. We can return it. Get it back where it belongs."

Piers nodded. "We have to get in touch with Little and Large's boss."

Sidney stepped back. "Their boss?"

"Yeah. You don't think we want to trust that pair, do you?"

"Well ..."

"No. We need to deal with their boss to make sure this gets handed over and that we're off the hook with these guys."

He watched as Sidney's nostrils flared and she clamped her jaw shut. She pushed her lips together so hard the pink almost disappeared. Then her smile returned and she put her arm through his. "You're right. Come on. Let's get away from here and sort it out."

"Riiight."

They walked out of the dead end and away from Notre Dame.

"We need to celebrate," Sidney said.

Piers tapped the tube. "After we've handed this thing over."

"It's not a thing, it's a precious painting. Either way, we need a good place."

They passed a couple of restaurants until they reached a sign that read Epicure. "This one," she said as she veered off into an expanse of tables set with white clothes fluttering in the wind. She talked to the maître d', and waved for Piers to follow as they disappeared into the restaurant.

His skin prickled. He licked his lips and looked up and down the street. For once, he wished he saw the familiar faces of Little and Large.

He breathed deep and followed Sidney. Her hair drifted from side to side as she walked. Even in the low heels she had chosen in Places des Voges, she walked with supreme grace. She weaved around the tables with a spring in her step that had been absent while they were searching the side roads. He sighed.

She was wonderful. Fabulously beautiful. Quick with a comeback. Sassy. Wise to the world. Exactly the sort of girl he dreamed about. But he wasn't hers. Even in the clothes she had picked for him, he was no different than he'd ever been. Same old, same old. Xbox on a Friday night. Beers at the pub, not dancing in clubs. They'd been a team for a few hours. Under pressure. Under duress. But it wouldn't last. Once the painting was handed over she would run a mile.

Sidney directed the woman to a table in the corner, behind a pillar. The maître d' looked surprised at her table choice, then handed them menus, and left. Piers placed the tube between himself and the wall, laying his arm across it for good measure.

Sidney flipped through the options in seconds. "Ratatouille. Plain and simple, just like me."

"You just ate a couple of hours ago."

"We found the painting. I've got my appetite back."

"Obviously."

She pulled the menu from Piers' hands. "Aren't you happy?"

He forced a smile. "Course."

She lowered her head and stared at him through her fringes. "Course? That's the best you can say? We found it. We're done. It's over. One moment we're in fear for our lives and the next, poof, we're back to normal. Surely that deserves some sort of celebration?"

"I'm only going be happy once we've handed this thing over."

Her smile faded. "Yes. Soon." She stood up. "Order for me. I'm going to the restroom." She walked away, fumbling her phone from her pocket.

Piers watched her go, hypnotized by the spring in her step and the motion of her silky dress.

"Monsieur?"

Piers lurched back to the real world and grabbed for the tube.

A young man with black pants and a starched white shirt stood beside the table. "You are ready to order, non?"

Piers looked the guy up and down and scanned the restaurant before speaking. "Ratatouille. Twice. And two glasses of red wine."

"Red?"

"Yeah, red."

The man turned over the menu. "We have many reds, monsieur, if you like." He paused, and his voice took on a bored tone, "Or we have the house red."

Piers snapped the menu shut. "That'll do."

The young man departed and Piers surveyed the restaurant before pulling out Auguste's phone. He turned to face the wall and dialed Little and Large.

Little answered on the first ring. "Where are you?"

"I never knew you cared."

"Don't get smart with me."

"The merest hint of an inkling of a thought hadn't even begun to start formulating in—"

"And don't do that either. We're on a tight schedule. The boss wants his stuff back."

"Ah, pronto, as you said."

"So?"

"So, what?"

"So, are you going to hand it back?"

"It's not as simple as that. There are things to consider. Options. Permutations. Probabilities—"

"And the likelihood that you'll be killed if you don't hand it over."

"So, you think we should hand it over?"

There was a long pause. "You mean ... you have it?"

"Uh-huh."

There was an even longer pause. "You sure?"

"Course I'm sure. We found Auguste's car and found it inside."

Piers heard Little take a deep breath. "Right."

"Right, what?"

"Right, just right, you know."

"Right."

Piers heard the pair talking in hushed tones before Little spoke into the phone again. "Okay. We need to let the boss know. Where are you?"

"Tell you boss we'll meet him at Epicure. It's a restaurant. We'll be sat outside. Be there at seven."

"No funny stuff."

Piers huffed. "Trust me, we want this over as much as you do."

"There's, er..."

"What?"

"Well, there's something, I mean—"

There was mumbling noises on the other end then Large came on the line. "You sure you've got the painting?"

"Definite."

"Good. Don't do anything clever. And don't mess with the boss. He isn't called Matchstick for nothing. And ..."

"And what?"

"He'll bring another crew."

Piers bit his lip. His heart raced and his mouth felt dry. He swallowed. "Meaning?"

"Not us. Trained killers. Real. Trained. Killers."

Piers took deep breaths and tried to slow his heart. "Right."

"Do what he says. To the letter. And you'll be all right."

"Yeah, thanks."

The phone went dead as Sidney returned to the table. "Did they call?"

"I called them. Seven o'clock. Outside. We hand over the painting and try to get our lives back."

"What?" Sidney grabbed her phone and checked the time. "Oh. Long enough."

The waiter returned with their meals and two glasses of red wine, which he handled with his fingertips, as if he might catch something from them.

Piers stared at Sidney. "Long enough for what?"

"To eat," she said, waving her fork.

The Ratatouille was good. The tomatoes and herbs had worked their way into the sliced vegetables to perfection.

"Good choice," he said, holding up a red-tinged slice of zucchini.

"My comfort food." She held up her glass. "Along with this."

He clinked his glass with hers. "To normality."

"Normality," she chorused.

They ate for a few moments before she spoke again. "This is a different Friday night, eh?"

He nodded and ate some more. "Yeah. I guess you go out with your ... I guess ... I mean do you ..."

She looked at him expectantly. "Do I what?"

He cleared his throat. "Do you ... do you have ... I mean ... do you have a boyfriend?"

She snorted. It was part amused and part contemptuous. Piers wasn't sure which part was in the majority.

"Nah. I go out with some girls I know," she said. "I'm done with men for a while."

"Oh."

She grunted. "It's not like that. I want to meet someone, just not drunk in a bar, you know? I want to get to know someone before I go out with him. The men I've met in bars have only been as faithful as their options."

Piers had to think for a moment before he understood. "Right."

She put another forkful of vegetables in her mouth. "What do you look for in a girl?"

He forced down a mouthful of ratatouille. "I … I don't really look—" he struggled to find words that didn't involve her. "I mean, I don't really know. I never thought about it."

"You have to think about it. You have to know what you want. You can't leave it to chance. You'll end up unhappy."

He nodded, uncertainly. "What do you want?"

She laughed. "A friend. Someone who stands up to me and doesn't say yes just because they think it'll make me happy. Because it won't. Neither of us will end up happy. I want someone who's willing to grab life, jump in with both feet. Someone who'll drag me along as much as I drag them. Someone who'll take me dancing before they think of dragging me to their bed. James Bond, but without the sappy floozies fawning all over him."

He gave a false laugh. "Well, that leaves me out. I've seen the movies, but I don't have the car."

She winked at him. "At least you have the accent." She curved her foot around his ankle and ran it slowly up his calf. "And you do have some muscles."

Piers tensed. The back of his neck prickled, and he licked his lips. "I, I work out. You know. A little. Cardio. Not for strength, just endurance."

She bit her bottom lip and smiled. "Mmmm, endurance …"

Piers swallowed and rubbed his hands together. He watched her gaze trace over his face, down his chest, and back up to his eyes. His blood thundered in his ears and the backs of his hands tingled. He wanted to get up, to cool down, to run away, to hide and think, to work out what he should say, to understand what he should do—but his muscles refused to cooperate. He was trapped between dying to say how he felt, and dying on the spot.

Sidney's phone dinged and her smiled dissolved. Her gaze drifted away. Piers felt his heart pause, waiting for her look back at him, hoping for the chance to say the right thing, to say anything that would prolong the moment. But she stared at her phone and muttered, "junk mail," before glancing around the room. "Six-thirty. We should have coffee."

Piers sighed. His shoulders sagged and he closed his eyes for a second. He felt as if a cold wind had blown over him. He had to open and close his mouth twice before his voice worked. "Coffee?"

"Yeah, coffee. People have coffee after dinner. At least this people does."

Piers arranged his knife and fork and pushed his plate away. His heart was pounding. He didn't want the meal to end, but he told himself he would feel better when they had got rid of the painting. They had to focus on that first. He took a deep breath. "Okay. Let's go outside."

"No, let's sit here."

He shook his head. "I told Little and Large we'd be outside."

"At seven o'clock, right?"

"Yeah."

"It's only six-thirty, so we can stay here a while longer."

Piers looked around the room. It was quiet, and perhaps they should keep out of sight as much as possible. "Okay."

A few minutes later, they chinked their coffee cups in a second toast. He sniffed at the thick black liquid. "I'm going to be up all night."

She laughed. "I was hoping we'd be able to go to bed."

Piers stopped breathing with his cup inches from his mouth.

She looked at him for a moment before laughing loud. "On our own. So wipe that look off your face."

His face felt on fire. "I'm sorry, I didn't... I wasn't—"

"It's okay, I'm teasing." She punched him playfully on the shoulder.

He shuffled in his seat. "Of course. I wasn't—"

The front door to the restaurant slammed and Sidney jerked her head up.

Piers twisted in his chair and saw an old couple being led to a table by the maître d'.

He looked back at Sidney. "Getting twitchy?"

"No, why should I?" She checked the time on her phone. "Still fifteen minutes yet."

Piers leaned back in his chair. They'd have to go outside soon, but he didn't want her doing anything rash. He took a deep breath. "There's one thing you need to know."

She turned her gaze slowly toward him. "What?"

"Little and Large warned me that their boss isn't one to be messed with."

She shrugged. "That's not exactly a surprise."

"And that he would be bring a different crew."

Sidney cheeks sagged. She spoke slowly. "Meaning?"

"Meaning trained killers. Real ones."

She slapped her hand to her forehead. "Oh, god! Why didn't you tell me? I thought it was going to be Little and Large, and now..."

"Now what?"

"Now... now ..." She shook her head. "This isn't good."

"Obviously. I've no desire to meet trained killers either. But we'll do it outside. On the street. With plenty of people around. That way they won't be able to do anything, you know?"

"Like kill us if things don't go their way?"

"Well—"

"Why the hell didn't you tell me earlier?" She looked at her phone and shook it, as if willing it for some kind of answer.

"I didn't want to frighten you."

"Great, so you leave it until the last minute, until it's a crisis." She started typing on her phone.

"What are you doing?"

She ignored him and finished her typing. Her phone dinged a moment later.

"Did you send a message to someone?"

"You're just full of questions this evening, aren't you?"

"Thinking ahead is what's kept us alive. It's why we're here with a chance to get our lives back. Did you send a message to someone?"

She glowered at him. "Get your life back, maybe. My life will be the same as ever. Men tramping in, walking all over me and buggering off."

"What do you mean? Are you talking about me?" He leaned forward. "Have I tramped all over you and buggered off?"

"We only met this morning, you haven't had the chance yet."

Piers clenched his jaw and breathed out hard. "Thank you very much, but don't evade the question. I want to know, Sidney. Did you send a message to someone?"

She stood up, crossed behind his chair and pulled the tube from beside him. She shook it in his face. "You don't know what this is or what it means to some people."

"So you do know something about it."

"I know enough to know it can't be replaced. I know enough to know a whole nation would be heartbroken if they knew it had been taken. I know enough to know what's important to a country's heritage."

"What are you talking about? Is this some kind of set up? Have you just been using me to find this painting?" He reached for the tube. She stepped away, whipping it behind her back. "All you care about is giving it to some murderous mob boss to save your own skin."

He stared in her eyes. "I'm trying to save yours, too. If you hadn't noticed."

"Yeah, right. Deflect the blame to keep your conscience happy. Just like you do with your mother."

"I do not—"

Sidney turned and ran from the restaurant. He jolted to his feet, sending his chair flying across the floor. He saw the maître 'd heading in his direction. He fumbled some notes from his wallet, threw them on the table, and ran after Sidney.

He stepped out onto the sidewalk. Two large men held Sidney, one arm apiece. Her eyes burned into Piers.

A man in a cream suit stepped forward. "I believe this is mine." He yanked the tube from Sidney's hands. She gave a faint "No," without looking at him.

"Morel?" said Piers.

The man turned to Piers. "So, you're lover boy, the one that helped steal this from me."

"We didn't steal it."

The man sneered. "No, no, of course you didn't. You and this girl just happened to know where to find it ... when my men tore this town apart looking for it and turned up nothing."

"It's not yours, anyway," said Sidney.

"Oh, I believe it is. I paid for it."

"You can't. It can't be bought, it's part of our national heritage."

The man huffed. "Our national heritage? You mean your national heritage."

Sidney struggled against the men holding her and they redoubled their grips.

Piers glanced from Sidney to the boss. "National heritage?"

The boss smiled at him. "How precious. Lover boy doesn't know." He gave a sneer, "She's not French. She's an immigrant. Illegal, in case you're wondering, which is why she didn't want to go to the police. They would have locked her up in an instant."

Piers looked at Sidney. "Really?"

Sidney's face froze, her lips parted and her eyes focused inches in front of her. She shuffled her weight from one foot to another. "Still not yours. It isn't anyone's to sell."

The man tapped the tube. "Sell? I wasn't selling. I paid for it. I bought this from your conniving dictator. Which brings us to my other interest." He turned to Piers, "Where did you claim to find this?"

Piers stiffened. "In Auguste's car. We worked out th—"

"Show me the car."

Piers glanced at Sidney, but she was looking up and down the street. Was she thinking of running? The two guys had a very firm grip on her, but maybe she was hoping to get free when they were walking? These guys had to be carrying guns, and Piers didn't fancy the idea of sprinting away from a hail of bullets.

The boss leaned forward, bringing his face inches from Piers'. His breath was filled with garlic and his eyes bored into Piers. "I said, show me the car."

Piers led them back to the dead end. He looked down the dimly lit road. It was an ideal hangout for muggers, only they were already hostages. He glanced behind and saw the boss, and behind him Sidney between the two men. What if Sidney did try to run? Would she get far? Maybe if she dodged between the cars so they wouldn't have a clear shot. He licked his lips and decided. If she ran, he would jump the men. Even a few moments' distraction would probably be enough for her to disappear into the crowds on the main road.

Sweat trickled down his back. He wriggled so his shirt would soak up his fear. Why did this guy want to see the car? Did he think he would find something else? What else could there be? Another painting? And what would Morel do if he did find something?

Piers stopped by the car.

"Open it," said the Morel.

Piers popped the handle and the door opened with a tinny clank.

Morel pushed past him and sat in the driver's seat. He looked over the glove box and rummaged in the central storage area. He twisted himself over to look under the seats, checked the rear of the car, then stepped out and glowered at Piers. "So where is—"

Piers heard weird ticking sounds behind him. As he rotated to look, Sidney screamed. One of the men holding her was falling to the ground, blood pouring down his face. The other man was already face down on the sidewalk.

Piers leapt for Sidney. "Get down!" He shoved her into the

side of the dumpster and onto the ground. She rolled, wrestling herself free of his grip. He heard boots pounding on the sidewalk and prayed it was the police.

Sidney stood up. Piers dived after her. The giant he had knocked down with the motorbike appeared around the corner of the yellow dumpster. Piers couldn't stop. The man threw one arm around Sidney and the other into Piers' face. The man's clenched fist smashed into his right cheek. Piers' head jerked backward and pain bloomed across his face. His momentum lifted him into the air, his arms thrashing in circles. His body hammered down on the sidewalk, squeezing every last gasp of air from his lungs.

He rolled onto his side, struggling to breathe and clutching his ribs. His face felt on fire and his head felt as if it was being shaken with a jackhammer. Another large man appeared behind Morel, and a third man in a long coat stepped in between them.

"You," Morel said.

"Now, now," said the man in the long coat.

"President Brunwald," said Sidney.

Piers looked at the man in the long coat and back at Sidney. "You know him?" He felt another force grip his chest. Brunwald? As in Brunwald the Butcher? The tyrant of Elbistonia?

Coughing, Piers rolled onto his knees. The giant holding Sidney pointed a large gun at him. "Don't even think about it."

Piers rolled back onto his side.

"Thank god you arrived," Sidney said, as she tried to worm free of the man's grip. "They were about to get away with the painting."

Piers glowered at Sidney.

"Your message reached us just in time, my dear," Brunwald said.

"You work for him?" Piers said.

Sidney glanced at him. "At least he's trying to recover our country's history, not sell it off like the man you work for."

"I don't work for anyone."

"Yeah, right, Mr. Waterloo construction guy. For a software engineer you did a great impression of Sherlock Holmes finding that painting."

"I—"

"That's enough," Brunwald said. He pulled the tube from the Morel's hands. "I believe this is mine."

"You took my money," Morel said.

Brunwald shook his head. "Your man, Auguste, he took the money, not me. He tried to double cross us both, and failed."

"Auguste would never double cross me."

"Really."

"He worked for me for twelve years. He never cheated, never disobeyed an order, and definitely never tried to take what wasn't his. Hell, he never even asked for a raise."

"And let me guess, you never offered one, either?"

Morel shrugged. "Why give someone something they haven't asked for?"

"So you were paying him the same for twelve years, and you don't see a problem with that?"

"I don't need some trumped-up dictator like you to tell me how to run my business."

Brunwald's face hardened. He spoke slowly. "Don't ever tell a trumped-up dictator that."

He turned back to Sidney and smiled. Behind him there was a small, sharp chug. The side of Morel's face exploded, splattering flesh and blood over Auguste's car.

Piers watched Morel slump sideway to the ground. He saw Sidney's eyes following, too. She looked at Brunwald, her mouth open as if to speak, but Brunwald waved a finger. "A constant thorn, my dear."

She swallowed. "You ... killed ... him."

"A precaution, my dear."

Brunwald turned to one of his men. "Get rid of them and search the car."

Sidney's mouth hung open. "You shot them."

Brunwald gave a sympathetic smile. "A necessary evil, I'm afraid. They were the worst of the worst, in many ways."

"But you shot them."

"They were greedy, my dear. That man wanted the painting and hoped to cheat his way out of paying for it. So now, he's paid for it."

She shook her head. "But you don't want anyone to pay for it. You're saving it to take home. Back to Elbistonia. For the country."

Brunwald placed his finger over his lips. Sidney's mouth kept moving, but no sound came out.

Brunwald's men threw the bodies into the giant dumpster, then turned to Auguste's car. They ripped out the seats, the carpets, and the dashboard. They tore the interior door panels out, peered into the engine compartment, and slashed open the tires. When they finished they stuffed the debris back into the car and slammed the doors. The giant shook his head. Brunwald pursed his lips and looked at Piers and Sidney.

Piers took a step forward. "We had nothing to do with those people. I'm just—"

Brunwald held his hand up. "I know, I know. A software engineer from England. Caught in a terrible mix-up. A real boo-hoo tragedy. And you're worried, quite correctly, that your life is in danger. It isn't a good story, but we may still be able to find a happy ending."

Sidney's mouth stopped moving and she regained her power of speech. "But we found the painting. It's in the tube. You have it."

"Yes, my dear. You've been invaluable in regaining the painting. You and your lover."

"I'm not her lover," said Piers.

Brunwald place a finger across his lips. "Both of you have served me well. There's just one more thing."

"But you wanted to recover the painting," Sidney said, "To take it back home, Elbistonia, where it belongs."

Brunwald gave a soft laugh. "My dear, the country is going to rack and ruin. Discipline is failing in the police and the armed services. There have been riots. People have been killed. Government buildings have been attacked. My own car was blown up. I am only thankful it was my wife, and not me, in it."

Brunwald crossed his hands behind his back. "No, there is no going back. I have done my utmost to serve my country. To bring order where there was chaos, and what do I get in return? Awards? Honors? Recognition? The thanks of a grateful nation? No, my dear. I have received none of these things. Not from Elbistonia, nor the international community. Therefore, there is only one thing left for me to do. Retire gracefully."

"But the painting."

"The painting is worthless."

Sidney looked puzzled. "It's a fake?"

"No, my dear. It is the real thing. However, I am forced to move quickly. I really must leave Europe for a country with, shall we say, less interest in extradition.

"So, you see, I don't actually want the painting. No, no, no. What I want is the money." He pointed to the dumpster. "The money that gentleman was going to pay for it."

"But you said you were looking for the painting to return it."

Brunwald forced his lips together into a thin flat line. "You are becoming something of a bore, my dear. I no more want the painting than I need you two alive."

Piers inched toward Sidney. One of the dictator's men pointed a silenced pistol at him and shook his head with a sneer. Piers froze.

"However." The dictator stepped toward Piers "It occurs to me that you have done well to find the painting, and I am a fair man. So, I will give you until midday tomorrow to find the money."

"We don't have it," Piers said.

"So you say." Brunwald nodded to the giant holding Sidney.

"You've met Kuznik, I believe. He isn't well known for his compassion. Or his patience."

The man pushed the barrel of his gun into the soft flesh under Sidney's chin. She gagged and squirmed. The man yanked her hair back until she stopped fighting.

Brunwald patted Piers on the shoulder. "You are a resourceful young man. I suggest you make a greater effort in your search. And be warned, if I have any indication you have contacted the police." Brunwald drew a finger across his throat. "You get the idea, I think."

Piers' heart pounded as if it was trying to jump from his chest. His voice trembled. "But we've searched his apartment, his safety deposit box, and his car. You've even searched his car. We haven't seen a hint of any money. What do you expect us to do?"

Brunwald smiled at Piers. "Why, find it, Mr. Chapman, find it. You have until midday tomorrow. No more. If you are unsuccessful, we will be forced to deposit your girlfriend outside Notre Dame. And I emphasize deposit."

"But I don't know where this money is. I haven't got a clue. There's nothing I can do. You can't be serious."

"I think you will find I am quite serious." Brunwald rapped his knuckles on the dumpster. "I would suggest you ask the previous people we dealt with on this issue but, of course, they are unavailable for comment."

Sidney squirmed away from the gun in her throat. "You bastard."

Brunwald laughed. "If, by that, you mean you have been foolish and gullible, and have undermined anything you and lover boy might have achieved together, my dear, you are correct. Your information has been invaluable. You were easily manipulated, but don't think badly of yourself. I have manipulated better people than you just as easily."

Brunwald's Mercedes tore down the street, J-turned, and

came to a stop beside him. Kuznik forced Sidney into the back, and Brunwald seated himself in the front.

Sidney leaned over Kuznik and looked up at Piers. She was biting her lip and tears streamed down her cheeks. "I ... I ... I'm sorry, I'm sorry. I didn't know ..." She wiped her nose on her sleeve. "You must hate me."

Piers' mouth hung half open. His face felt numb. His eyes were frozen, staring yet almost unable to see her. "No. Not hate. I didn't ..." He shook his head and forced his jaw to move and his voice box to speak. "I didn't do this, any of it... not because I hate you."

Her lower lip trembled. He reached for her and she stretched out her hand, but Kuznik yanked it back and closed the window. Piers watched Sidney dissolve into tears.

Brunwald tapped his watch. "Midday," he flicked a card out of his window. "Don't be late."

Piers glimpsed a phone number as the card fluttered to the sidewalk, and the car raced away.

CHAPTER TWENTY-TWO

Piers paced away from Notre Dame in a daze. People veered around him as if his shock was somehow contagious. He crossed two roads without looking before a car's horn pulled him up. He stood in front of the vehicle, gawping as the driver waved a fist. He stumbled back onto the sidewalk as the car screeched away, and stood on the curb, oblivious to the traffic inches from him.

They had taken her. Pushed her into their car and driven her away. Had she been working for Brunwald all along? Had she been playing him? The smile, the hugs, the moments in the shower? Was it all part of a plan that he had been stupid enough to fall into? Or had Brunwald used her as he was trying to use them both now? If you could call threatening a life, using.

He shook his head. No. It wasn't possible. They'd met by chance. He'd been the one to drive her away from the scene of Auguste's death. And her mood swings certainly didn't seem like she was trying to ingratiate herself.

He sighed as he remembered the moment in Place des Vosges when she stepped out of the dressing room wearing that dress. How it shimmered and danced around her figure. How she embraced him as they hid from the police behind the umbrella. He let out a single breathy laugh, but felt like he had been punched in the gut. She had been maddening, infuriating, moody. Yet, she had been exciting, vibrant, and thrilling. She was heartbreaking, and heartbreakingly beautiful. He should have said as much to her. He should have told her of his feelings. He should have risked that embarrassment. But he hadn't even known his own feelings. Not then, only now. But nothing mattered now. They had taken her. She was gone.

He leaned against the window of a store and rolled his head back. They'd found the painting and still Brunwald had taken her. Somehow, he'd duped her. Her text messages must have been reporting their progress. He must have known everything. He'd had the upper hand all the time, and Piers hadn't even known he existed. He'd even waited until the mob to showed up, so he could dispense with them without a second thought. Piers swallowed. He didn't want to find her body in front of Notre Dame.

A fine drizzle misted his face. The drops glittered in the street lamps, a sparkling carpet in the air. The foot traffic on the streets thinned, the evening rush hour waning. Fewer people for him to hide among, fewer people to spot him. He walked toward the river, head down, sheltering from the rain.

His only way to get her back was to find the money Morel had been going to hand over for the painting. But how? What clues did he have?

He crossed another street, barely looking at the traffic.

There was always the police. Even though Brunwald had warned him against going to them, it was the sensible idea. It was the idea they should have gone with at the start. His idea. The police could have sorted all this out, even if they had been placed in cells until it was done. Being in a cell with a bed and three meals a day was a much better prospect than being wanted on the streets with—he swallowed—her being held hostage.

Hostage? What was he thinking about? He needed to go to the police. Now. He scanned the street for a gendarme. Why hadn't he gone to them before? No matter what happened to him, they could sort this out. They would have the resources. They probably had cameras everywhere, like London. They could trace Brunwald and mount a raid, or surround his hideout and demand Sidney's release. As much as the man had shown no remorse for killing, he wasn't stupid. He'd let her go if he thought he might get away with it.

A police car turned onto the street ahead of him. He raised his hand. They would be able to save her. They would be able to capture Brunwald and bring him to justice. The police car showed no signs of slowing. Piers stepped out into the road and waved. Brunwald and his men had killed the mobster and his men, along with Auguste. The police couldn't help but see that. Piers would have to convince them, but it'd be worth it. Sidney only had until tomorrow. Midday tomorrow. He couldn't risk her life. It was the sensible thing to do.

But tomorrow? He brought his arm down a fraction. What if he couldn't convince them by midday? What if they pinned the murders on him? He whipped his arm down, and stepped back onto the sidewalk.

Murder! How could he convince anyone that he wasn't responsible? They had pictures of him on a motorbike running from the scene of Auguste's murder. And what if they had footage of him walking into the alley with Morel and then walking out without him? He sank to his knees and lowered his head into his hands. The police car didn't stop.

He exhaled. He was a software engineer, not a criminal mastermind. How was he supposed to solve this? If he went to the police he'd be done for. And if he didn't convince them to look for Sidney, she'd be dead by midday tomorrow. But if he didn't go to the police how was he supposed to find her? Or the money?

And what if Morel was trying to con Brunwald out of the painting? Maybe the whole affair with Auguste had been a ploy to steal the painting from Brunwald all along? Maybe the money never existed? Maybe, maybe, maybe. He ducked into the covered entranceway of a department store. There were so many questions, and he was out of his depth.

He rotated his head and shoulders, and stretched out his back. He had no clues, and the light was fading fast. Not that he knew what he was going to do anyway. He stepped out from under the shelter of the building. The fine rain, which had felt refreshing before, now felt miserable.

Across the street, a light flickered into life. A sign. Big and bold. He felt as if a blanket of cold engulfed him, sweeping the air from his body. The single word *Bernard's* glowed in purple neon script above a white canopy. It was Sidney's nightclub, the place she had wanted to hide for the night. The place she had wanted to take him. The girl who just wanted to have fun. The girl he had turned down. Seeing the name was like a physical blow. Why hadn't he said yes? Why hadn't they gone there? Why hadn't he asked her to dance? She even said she wouldn't leave him.

He sighed. It was too late now. No amount of begging in the world would bring her here now. He felt for the tickets Sidney had given him. They were stiff card, laminated, with *Bernard's* embossed in the same color and swoopy font as the glowing neon across the street. On the back someone had written "free admittance" with a stylized "B" underneath. The man himself, presumably.

A line had already formed beneath the neon, early for a nightclub. Two bouncers stood in front of a white door. A rope had been placed along the sidewalk and patrons were rapidly assembling. A Bentley pulled up alongside the canopy. One of the bouncers rushed forward with an umbrella and sheltered a well-dressed couple that emerged from the rear. Flashes went off as the couple dived for sanctuary behind the white door.

Piers turned the tickets over in his hands. Sanctuary? He needed sanctuary. He needed time. Time to sit and think. Perhaps Sidney had been onto something. He squeezed the tickets. At least no one would recognize him in the dark of a nightclub.

He flipped up his collar and strode across the road for the canopy and its white door, ignoring the queue of people, confident in his ticket. Bernard's name would surely grant him instant access and, if it didn't, they'd just send him to the back of the line. No big deal. No problem. Nothing to worry about.

At least, that was what he thought. Right up until he saw the bouncers talking to a gendarme.

CHAPTER TWENTY-THREE

Piers sweated. Surely the police wouldn't be checking nightclubs in their search for him and Sidney? There again, Sidney had said she knew the owner, so perhaps they were checking places she was known.

The gendarme stared at Piers as he approached. He couldn't turn around now. His shirt clung to him. It was make or break time. Should he walk away? Rush off as if he'd just remembered something? Or could a run-in with the law really be the best twist of fate?

The bouncers waved people through the entrance in small groups. He slowed his pace and joined the rear of a gaggle of noisy girls.

One of the bouncers held out his arm, deftly cutting off Piers from the girls. "Monsieur?"

Piers held up his ticket. The man glowered at it. Behind him the gendarme went quiet.

The bouncer didn't blink. "You have a ticket."

Piers shook the ticket.

The bouncer frowned. "Oui, monsieur. And this ticket was given to you by?"

Piers' heart pounded his rib cage. "Bernard."

The man nodded. "Ah, Bernard."

Piers smiled big. "Oui, Bernard."

The bouncer plucked the ticket from Piers hand. "Bernard doesn't give tickets to single men, Monsieur."

Piers licked his lips. "He ... he didn't. He gave these tickets to my girlfriend. And me."

"Ahhhh, and your girlfriend is?"

Damn. Dare he mention Sidney's name? What if the gendarme had just alerted the bouncers to her name? He swallowed. "Busy."

The doorman's shoulders sagged and he gave an exasperated sigh. "Her name, monsieur."

"Oh," Piers tipped his head forward and spoke in a low voice. "Sidney."

The doorman's face coiled into a left-handed sneer. "Sidney? You? You're her boyfriend?"

The gendarme took a step to one side, to gain a better view. Piers felt sweat trickle down his back. Was this it? Was this where he was going to be arrested? Sneaking into a Paris nightclub? He focused on the bouncer. He had to think like the French. He shrugged. "This week, oui. But next week? Who can tell?"

The man snorted a laugh. "So, when does she get here?"

Piers waved his hands in the air. "Thirty minutes? An hour? Who knows?"

The man slapped the ticket back into Piers' hand. "Go on."

Piers took the ticket and opened the door, but the gendarme called "Wait."

Piers' heart skipped a beat. His skin prickled. He turned slowly around. The man was pointing his finger at his watch. "This week is almost over."

Piers face felt numb. "And?"

"So, your week is almost up. Better make the most of tonight, yes?" He had a lascivious grin and gave a theatrical wink. "It may be your last."

The gendarme erupted into laughter. Piers' heart resumed beating and the numbness in his face melted into a broad grin. "Oui, oui, tonight." He let the door slip from his fingers and disappeared into the club, wiping sweat from his brow.

A flight of stairs descended onto a gantry above a giant underground dance floor. In opposite corners, bars were doing a brisk trade, but the floor was mostly empty. A DJ stared down from a platform raised above the floor. Lasers, lights, and LEDs pulsed around the room. Lines and shapes spun over the ceiling and floor. Samples of Duran Duran mixed with heavy dance music pounded from speakers hung from the ceiling. Along one side he saw booths set into the wall like Stone Age caves. He got a beer from the bar and headed for one, sliding into the back to watch the entrance and the dance floor.

He cradled his beer. What would it have been like if they had come here? Would she have talked all night? Danced like crazy? Both, probably. Only now he'd never know. He breathed in deeply and straightened himself up. At least, he'd never know if he failed her.

A man in a cream suit walked across the floor toward him. He waved at some of the dancers as he crossed the open space, then seated himself directly opposite Piers. "I hear you're waiting for Sidney."

Piers' eyes narrowed. "You know her?"

The man leaned across the small table. "I gave her those tickets."

"You're Bernard?"

"You're English. And, pardon me for saying this, an unlikely person to be in possession of those tickets. You don't seem like Sidney's type."

"And what type do you think she goes for?"

Bernard shrugged. "Not, monsieur, a man who sips beer on his own in a corner."

"I'm not having a good day."

Bernard leaned forward. "Let me give you some advice about

Sidney. She's a true Parisienne. The type of person she would go for doesn't sulk about not having a good day. He grabs it by the throat and changes the day."

Piers raised his gaze and started at Bernard. "She's not French. She's Elbistonian."

Bernard raised his head up. "Ah, so you do know her. This is good. And true." He thumped his chest. "But inside."

"Maybe."

"Definitely." Bernard stood up. "Monsieur, you may have the clothes to impress, but if you want to win Sidney, you will change the day."

Piers watched him walk away, talking to patrons, passing from group to group, waving at a couple on the dance floor. He was calm, confident, assured—everything Piers didn't feel about himself.

He toyed with his beer. Should he search Auguste's apartment again? Find April? Neither of those would be easy. Certainly not before midday tomorrow.

He stretched. What else could he do? Contact Little and Large? Where had they gone? They'd tipped him off about Morel bringing other men, but what could he get out of them?

The only thing left was Auguste's car. He took a mouthful of beer. He didn't relish the idea of returning to a murder scene, or the place where he'd last seen Sidney, but Bernard was right.

If he wanted to win Sidney, he had to change the day.

CHAPTER TWENTY-FOUR

Outside Bernard's, the gendarme had moved on. Piers walked along the line of well-dressed patrons. They eyed him curiously, unsure why someone would leave the club so early, or maybe wondering he if resembled the man on the motorbike.

Streetlights glowed through the misty drizzle, and the night air felt good on his face again. Neons lit up hotel signs, and light from shop windows spilled onto the road. He blew out a long breath. If the painting had been the answer to their problems, it would have been a wonderful night to be in Sidney's company. Even when she'd made his blood boil, she'd lit up the world.

He arrived at the entrance to the dead end. The street looked dark, the city economizing on street lamps. He bought a large aluminum flashlight from a pharmacy on the corner and headed into the street's gloom. He walked in the center of the road, keeping away from the doorways, and stretching his shoulders and flexing his fingers. He kept the flashlight off, gripping it with his right hand and slapping it satisfyingly into his left. It had a good heft and he found the idea of fighting a mugger strangely appealing.

But he didn't need to work out his aggression, he needed get Sidney back, and to get Sidney back he needed to find the money. He slapped the flashlight into his palm. Yes, he had to get her back. The dictator had men and guns, but he didn't have the money. That was all he wanted, and that was the only thing that would save her.

Piers' mouth went dry as he approached the giant dumpster. Brunwald had thrown Morel and his men in them, and they were undoubtedly dead, but he still had misgivings. He gave the yellow monster a wide berth.

Auguste's car looked unloved. The seats had been wrenched free of their moorings and the carpets were stuffed into the driver's seat. The dashboard had been pulled forward and the carpet in the rear hatchback was missing, exposing the spare tire and tire lever. Worst of all, dark patches on the roof testified to Morel's violent end.

Piers flipped on the flashlight. Bullet holes glinted around the rear of the car. Auguste had been shot at while he was escaping from Gare de l'Est. The shots had been aimed low, and none of the glass in the car was broken. It seemed absurd, but perhaps the dictator's men were trying to keep a low profile. Blowing the glass out in the car certainly would have brought plenty of attention in the street.

The door opened with a jolt and a clang. A large chunk of dashboard dropped to the ground. He stuffed it back into the car and sat on the dislodged driver's seat. His flashlight caught two bullet holes in the dashboard.

He placed his hands on the steering wheel and twisted to stare out of the rear window. Auguste had been running from the fight at Gare de l'Est, probably driving like a madman while being shot. He'd been heading to Montparnasse station. He'd probably planned to take the direct route, then been forced into weaving though streets to throw off his attackers. He'd lived in Paris, so he'd have known the route better than Brunwald's men.

Piers looked out of the driver's side window and down the street. So, why turn into a dead end? He stepped out of the car. The gunmen would have been on his tail, yet he purposely trapped himself. If Auguste knew the roads in the area, surely he could have shook them off in other streets without turning into a dead end?

Piers walked the last thirty feet down the street. A tall, white, wooden barrier blocked his way. It was secured to the walls of the buildings on either side, leaving no way to pass. He shone his flashlight over the temporary wall. A large sign apologized for the disruption in several languages. A single name was written underneath. He didn't have to sweep the light across the length of the name to know what it said. It was expected and unexpected. In large, neat, Courier script, the words "Waterloo Large Construction" blazed into the night.

He pulled up a map of the area on his phone. The road zigzagged to another that led across the Seine and onto Montparnasse. Beyond the white barrier lay the building project his company had been contracted to help construct.

Piers stuffed his phone back into his pocket. No wonder Auguste had spat at him when he saw the Waterloo emblem on his shirt. Auguste had turned down this street believing he could shake off his pursuers, but Waterloo had blocked off the street the day before. They'd put up the white barriers, moved in the cranes, and sent Piers to fix the software. There was no way Auguste could have known Waterloo would foil his escape.

Piers looked back at the car. It was pointing toward the white barrier. Auguste had dumped the car when he saw the barrier and continued on foot. But where? Back past the pharmacy? That would have meant passing the gunmen chasing him. He swung the flashlight over the walls lining the sides of the street. There were no alleyways to access other streets. Piers bit his lip. What would he do if people were shooting at him? The answer was simple, run. And he only had one choice.

Piers swung his light over the tall white barricade. The warning sign was attached with large wooden blocks that might give purchase. He pulled himself up, wary of a steep drop on the other side.

Balanced on the top of the wall he saw that the site was deserted. Serious construction hadn't started yet. The cranes stood silent in opposite corners, a Portakabin between them. The surface layer of the area had already been removed, leaving mud everywhere.

Directly below him, the ground sloped down to a large pit that took up half the site, excavation for the foundation of the building Waterloo was to construct. The rain had turned the pit into a lake filed with thick brown water. He focused the beam from the flashlight directly below him and saw the smooth surface of the muddy slope was pockmarked in a line that descended into the water. Auguste's path, perhaps? He examined the far side of the lake and saw similar marks leading down into the water. Or, more likely, one set of marks led in, and the other led out, because if Auguste had jumped this wall while running from his attackers, he'd have fallen straight into the lake.

Piers inched his way along the top of the wall, away from the pit, lowered himself down, and jumped the last five feet. His shoes were sucked into the thick mud. He levered them out and fought his way to the other side of the lake.

Along the side of the lake he found a broad net, secured at the top of the slope with large stakes and running down into the water. Waterloo's idea of safety in case anyone fell in, and cheaper than a night watchman.

On the far side of the lake, footprints were clearly dug into the sloping side of the pit and continued to a metal ladder running up the side of the Portakabin. The building was locked and empty, yet to be filled with the mass of paperwork that followed a construction project. He climbed the ladder onto the roof.

The Portakabin was only a foot from another white temporary wall at the opposite side of the site. Piers ran his flashlight across it and a large stain, dark red and thigh-high, confirmed the route Auguste had taken.

Piers looked over the wall and its dark stain to a cobblestone alleyway below. An old couple hurried by. He checked the map on his phone. The alley led to the square in front of Notre Dame, the place where they had all met in that fateful taxi.

So, where had the money gone? If Auguste had taken it from his car, it was gone by the time he reached the taxi. Piers looked back down the alleyway. A group of men walked by, drunk and singing. If Auguste had dropped a bag of money in the lane, it would have been found long ago. The same went for the area around Notre Dame, and it certainly wasn't in his car. Piers shone the flashlight around the building site. It was nothing but mud with one line of footprints. Auguste had run in and straight out. What options were left?

He walked back to the pit and knelt down by the safety netting to scan the surface of the lake. In the faint nighttime glow of moon and streetlights, he saw sheets of rain dimpling the surface with lines that bucked and twisted at the wind's whim. He marveled that even in the cloying mud and winter cold, nature could reveal its beauty everywhere.

Everywhere, save one small square in the middle of the lake.

CHAPTER TWENTY-FIVE

The small square drifted in the murky water, only visible by its effect on the rain splashing the water. Whatever it was, it was thoroughly sodden and the weight of adsorbed water was keeping it just below the surface.

He untied a plastic rope from one side of the safety netting and scoured the building site for something to float. He found a large plastic carrier bag advertising a chain of shops, hooked the rope through the handles, inflated the bag, and knotted it.

With a few minutes perseverance, he floated the bag to the square and dragged the object back to the lake's edge. He pulled a filthy briefcase from the water and cradled it in his hands as a dirty slurry drained out. The sides flexed. The last thing he needed was for it to break open and to have to retrieve the contents from the muddy ground.

He looked around the site. The Portakabin was locked and the only other structures were the two giant cranes in the far corner. They had huge concrete bases that served as foundations to stabilize the giant machines. He looked up and saw the operator's cabin at the top of the crane and kicked himself for being so stupid.

He pulled his phone from his pocket, entered the web

address for the Waterloo site, and chose the "Engineering login" button. A password later and he saw a list of all the cranes Waterloo had operational around the world. The cranes unique ID was stenciled in giant letters on the tower. Moments later he had control of the fifty-ton monster. All it took was one button press to bring the operator's cabin down to ground level.

The cabin wasn't large, but it was dry. Piers rested the case on a small fold-down table. The locks were secure, but he pried the weakened sides apart easily. Mud oozed out and he tilted the case to pour it away from him. A thick plastic bag took up all the space inside. He lifted it up. It was heavy and seam-welded at each end. Wiping it with his hand, he could see the inside was dry.

And filled with diamonds.

CHAPTER TWENTY-SIX

Piers had never seen loose diamonds. He hefted the bag. It was ten pounds at least. The plastic was thick. There was no way it was going to break open. He had no idea how much they were worth, but he was sure he'd never held so much money in his life. He shivered. That made him a target.

He looked over the building site. The plastic bag he had used to retrieve the case flapped in the breeze. He scanned the top of the temporary wall. What if Brunwald's men were watching?

He pulled his phone out and selected a couple of buttons on the crane's web page. After a moment, a buzzer sounded, then the cabin started to rise back to the top of the tower. The ground fell away, bringing the pit and its lake into clearer view. He could see the fine rain misting far streetlights. The angle of the lights and the buildings confused his senses. He grabbed the seat cushion and closed his eyes to fight off a wave of nausea.

The cabin jolted to a stop. He opened one eye, looking out as far away as he could until his balance felt good. In the distance he could see the Eiffel Tower, the white dome of the Sacré-Cœur, and an endless string of headlights weaving their way through the city. Beside him, the Seine gave distorted reflections of the lights on the opposite bank.

He turned over the bag. Somewhere out there, Brunwald the Butcher was holding Sidney and waiting for his call. Piers wished he could throw the diamonds and hit the man. The crane was a hundred and fifty feet tall and dropping something on him from that height was all Brunwald deserved.

Piers looked at the phone number the dictator had given him. No doubt it was a drug dealer special, bought at some corner store and activated anonymously. He wanted to demand Sidney's freedom, he wanted her back as soon as possible, he wanted rid himself of the fear and doubt. He pulled out his phone and his finger hovered over the buttons. He wanted all these things, but Brunwald would want to see evidence of the diamonds before he released Sidney.

Piers lowered the phone. Brunwald had killed the mob's men without a second thought. Once he had the diamonds, Sidney would be unnecessary—a liability, even. One that he would be quick to dispense with. Yet he wouldn't hand Sidney over without the diamonds.

Piers' phone beeped, the crane's web application closing down after a predetermined timeout. He watched an animation of the crane morphing into a puppy and bounding off the side of the screen. It was a stupid image for a machine capable of lifting tens of tons, and he'd told the designer, but the animation remained.

He looked out to the east where the crane's twin stood, dark and silent. A short distance beyond it the yellow of another large dumpster glowed in the night. He tapped a few buttons on his phone's browser, logged into the twin, and cycled the cabin lights. He had control of both cranes. No surprise, really, as he had come to Paris to update their software.

He looked down at the water's edge. The embankment road was two lanes wide in each direction. A small road dipped steeply off to what looked like a rarely used docking area for small craft. He strained around the back of his seat and saw the road came to an abrupt end. A dead end, like the one that had trapped Auguste.

He dialed Little and Large's number. It rang, then clicked over to an automated message saying the person he had called was busy. It didn't give an option to leave a message. He hung up and dialed again. On the fourth try, Little answered. "Get lost, we're busy."

"How well do you know your boss?"

"What kind of question is that?"

"It's my question to you. How well do you know him?"

Little snorted. "Well enough. We're, er, connected, you know."

"Connected? As in family?"

"Er ... "

"What do you do for him?"

"Look, it's very nice talking to you, but I've got important things to do."

"They've got Sidney."

"Who's got Sidney? The boss?"

"Your boss is in a dumpster in a back alley."

There was a long pause. "What?"

"You heard me. Him and his henchmen."

Another long pause. "What?"

"Him and his henchmen were killed by Brunwald the Butcher, and thrown in a dumpster."

"What?"

"Then Brunwald took Sidney. And if you say what again, I'm going to hit you."

Piers could make out the muffled sounds of a short argument then Large came on the phone. "Brunwald the Butcher, as in the dictator?"

"The very one."

"In Paris?"

"He was selling the painting to Morel. He killed Morel and wants the money Morel was going to pay for it."

"Let me guess, he's holding Sidney until you find it?"

"I need help."

"You need the police. Army even. Rumor is, Brunwald uses special forces to do his dirty work."

"My face is connected with a string of dead bodies."

Large paused. "We're not hit men, if that's what you think."

Little started talking excitedly in the background. Large covered the mouthpiece, and when he came back, Little was silent.

"We do cars," Large said. "That's all we do. We don't even work for Morel. My friend here is a distant relative. He just hired us to follow you for a while."

Piers hummed.

"What's he going to do with Sidney?" said Large.

"I don't know. He didn't show any hesitation when he shot Morel and his two men."

"He shot both of them?"

"You know them?"

"Just by reputation. They weren't the sort of people you'd want to cross."

"Brunwald had several men."

"We can't take them on. Like I said, we just do cars."

Piers bit his lips. "I need a car."

"You going to get out of the city?"

"No! I need to get Sidney back."

"What sort of car?"

"Something used. Medium size. Something that doesn't stand out."

"I know where I can get hold of an old blue Citroën. One with a big engine."

"Thanks."

"Do you have a plan?"

"Not sure. Can you get a boat?"

"Where?"

"The Seine."

Large exhaled. "Could do. Boat's not a good idea. Too easy to get caught. Nowhere to hide on the water. Not like with a car."

"Okay."

"Be about an hour for the car."

Piers hung up and looked down at the Seine. Large was right, it wouldn't be easy to escape from a madman with a gun at boat speeds. He breathed out deep and corrected himself. It was madmen, not madman.

His phone bleeped as the web interface timed out on the second crane. The stupid dog ran off the side of the screen, nothing like Rover's exuberant obedience.

He turned the phone over in his hand and despised the animation's creator one more time, but the cranes were an amazing power to be controlled from something so small.

He pulled up a map of the area. The embankment road was there, the bridges were there, the Seine was there, even the small road was there. A dilapidated building stood where the building site and cranes now stood.

He shone the flashlight out into the night, straight along the massive frame of the jib, then down to the end of the thick cables. He recognized the dual-pronged device on the end as the attachment that connected to the dumpsters. He grinned. The cranes had been used to move the giant dumpsters into position. With the right instructions, they could move them again.

He redialed Little and Large's number.

Little answered. "What?"

"I'm going to need something else."

"What do think we are? Amazon.com? Ow—"

Large came on the phone. "Got a plan now?"

"Yes, but I need something else. Scuba gear. A mask, oxygen, and flippers."

"One lot or two?"

"Just one."

"When do you need it?"

Piers thought for a moment. "Before dawn."

"No problem. Where do you want to meet?"

"Near Notre Dame."

"There's a twenty-four-hour café on Rue de Gascony. Terry's All Time. Go inside. Meet you there at 4am."

"Thanks."

"Watch your back."

Piers hung up, lowered the cabin to the ground, and clambered over the temporary wall and back out of the building site.

The dead-end street was as dark as ever. He ignored his sense of foreboding and pulled up the map on his phone. His GPS position appeared in the corner and he counted off the northings and eastings as he walked back and forth past the center of the dumpster. Satisfied, he worked his way around the block to where the second dumpster lay and went through the same routine.

Across the river, Notre Dame was lit up. He found the small road and noted the GPS position of the sloped entranceway. A dirty sign read Petit Quai. The road was really just a poor man's dock, a good ten feet lower than the main road. A rusty chain ran along the edge with two gaps, obviously intended for embarkation. The road was concrete, covered with equal parts oil, gravel, and moss. Its neglect contrasted jarringly with the care taken over its famous neighbor, but as Piers stood in the darkness he knew it was perfect.

He walked downstream to Pont au Double. The bridge's central stone support had a ledge a couple of feet above the water. The Seine burst into a small wake as it flowed around the support. Even in the lurid glow of the street lamps the water looked thick and dirty. A foam of green scum piled up against the stone of the bridge.

He timed his walk from Pont au Double downstream to Pont Saint-Michel at four minutes. The second bridge had similar stone pillars. Rusty metal hoops led down to the water. The river churned as it wound unhappily around the stone obstruction. He dropped a leaf and watched it roll below the murky surface in moments. The current was strong. He bit his lip and hoped his weight would help. Either way, he would know by the time he reached here whether his plan had worked. All he had to do was be patient.

He walked off the bridge and headed back to Bernard's to kill six hours.

CHAPTER TWENTY-SEVEN

The duct tape cut into Sidney's wrists, and the gag across her mouth forced her to breathe through her nose. She stretched her back and twisted her hips, almost the only thing she could move. Her legs were numb from lying in the same position for hours. She kept flexing her hands to ward off pins and needles.

Kuznik walked into the bedroom and smiled a broad, greasy sneer. His eyes darted from side to side, and Sidney wondered if he was on drugs, or if the thrill of seeing her bound on the floor did it for him.

He closed the door, the latch clicking softly behind him. She had no idea of the time, but there was no light around the heavy drapes. God, don't let her time be up. Or Piers' time, or whatever it was.

He smiled with one side of his face. "Comfortable down there?"

She glowered at him.

He walked around the room. "You know he hasn't called?"

Sidney grunted. Piers would call. He was clever. He'd find the money. And if he didn't, he'd bring the police. It was what he'd wanted to do in the first place. And they should have.

Kuznik stared at her and shrugged. "Maybe he won't call. Maybe he'll just leave you here."

Sidney clenched her teeth. He'd call. He had to call. He wouldn't leave her, would he? Could he? She sighed silently because she knew she had given him good reason to.

Kuznik sat on the bed, his boots inches from her face. "When we left him, I don't think he even managed to pick up the phone number. Think it blew away." He grinned. "That would make it difficult to call."

She screwed her face up and glowered at him. "He'll call," she grunted through her sealed lips.

"What's that you say? I can't quite hear you? Such a strange accent for a French person." He laughed.

Sidney lowered her head toward her chest.

He flexed his boots then reached down to touch her hair. "He is a coward. He didn't even try to get you free when we first arrived on the scene." He gazed up at the ceiling in mock contemplation. "And you know, if he didn't get you free then, why would he come back now?"

Sidney jerked her body in defiance.

The man rolled off the bed and knelt beside her. He ran his hand up her thigh. "Mind you." She jolted back the few inches that her bonds would allow, though not enough to stop him running his hand further up her thigh. "We could have some fun if he never came back."

The dictator's voice sounded at the door. "Leave her."

Kuznik looked up. His eyebrows inched together then his face took on a calm, neutral smile.

Sidney squeezed her knees up to her chest and let loose with all the might her bound legs could muster. Her stockinged feet thumped into Kuznik's side. He grunted, twisting to absorb the force, and swung his arm around, smacking her legs away.

He stood up, massaging his side with one hand and drawing his knife with the other. "Bitch!"

"We need her," Brunwald hissed.

Kuznik glanced at the dictator, slid his knife back into its sheath, and looked down at her. “You’re never going to see that creep again. And I am going to have some fun with you.”

He spat at her and walked out. The dictator followed, closing the door after him, like a parent escorting a child to bed.

Sidney’s heart slowed its race. She twisted her head to wipe the sweat off her brow with the carpet. Kicking him had been a stupid thing to do. She’d probably hurt herself more than him, and if Brunwald hadn’t turned up she might be dead. Not that she had much to thank Brunwald for. She’d fallen for his smooth lines, just like she fallen for so many other men’s smooth lines.

She sighed. Her chest felt heavy. She eased her head down onto the floor. If she could sum Piers up in one word, it would be sensible. No smooth lines, no saying what he thought she wanted to hear. Just the truth. The facts. The sensible options. If she was going to be freed, that was what she needed now. The sensible option.

All she could do now was hope Piers knew what is was.

CHAPTER TWENTY-EIGHT

Piers left Bernard's at three-thirty in the morning. The place was jumping. During the course of his hours at the bar, he'd been propositioned by both sexes and in three different languages. As the night had worn on he started to take it as a sport.

Terry's All Time was to the west, but he knew Brunwald would track his phone, so he headed east before calling the dictator. The phone was answered on the first ring. Kuznik's voice rasped slowly from the speaker. "What?"

"I want to talk to Brunwald."

"Whatever you've got to say to him, you can say to me."

"I'm not going to talk to the monkey when I want to talk to the organ grinder."

"Don't mess with me. My knife is one door away from the love of your life."

Piers swallowed. "Put him on, or I hang up."

"You better have good news or I'm going to open that door and mix things up with that bitch."

"Put him on."

There was a silence long enough to make Piers check his phone to see the call was still connected. Finally, Brunwald spoke. He was as smooth and polished as ever. "I hear you have something for me."

"As long as you have something for me."

"I'm a man of my word."

"I want to talk to her."

Brunwald hummed. "After you tell me what you've found."

"Diamonds."

"Excellent. And where did you found the diamonds."

"Abandoned at a building site."

Brunwald hummed. "My men must be losing their touch. How much do these diamonds weigh?"

Piers sweated. He wasn't good at guessing weight. "Ten pounds. Thereabouts. They're sealed in a thick plastic pouch."

"And where are you now?"

"Put Sidney on."

Brunwald sighed. There was a long silence finally broken by Sidney's voice. "Piers?"

"You okay?"

There was a long pause. "Kind of."

"You're going to be all right."

"I'm really sorry, I really am. Don't do anything stupid. Go to—"

The phone was wrenched away from her, but Piers heard the word "police" before Brunwald came back on.

"Very sweet, but we need to get down to business. Where are you?"

"You know Petit Quai?"

"No."

"Then buy a map and meet me there at 9am."

"No. We meet now."

"I need to sleep. Be there at nine. Bring Sidney and have your phone with you."

"One hint of a problem—"

"Just be there." Piers hung up. He was sure they had been

tracking his calls, and hoped they had got a good fix on his direction. He turned around and sprinted for Terry's All Time.

Twenty minutes later, sweaty and panting, he arrived at the sad sight of Terry's twenty-four-hour restaurant. The windows were thick with grime, and the door had come from a different building and been fitted badly. There was no sign of a blue Citroën parked on the street. Perhaps they had gotten something different. He felt a pang of guilt at the thought of someone being deprived of the car, but it was a necessary evil. Perhaps he could make it up to the owners afterward.

Inside, the café was as grimy as its windows. At the rear of the room, swing doors led into a kitchen where he could see steam rising from pots on a cooker.

To Piers' surprise, the café was full. Men talked in muted voices in groups huddled around small tables. Some wore jeans and some were dressed in cheap suits. None of them looked like hygiene was a top priority in their daily routine. The voices stopped when the badly-fitted door slammed shut behind him. He gave an uncertain smile to the faces that turned to look over the stranger in their midst, and headed for the counter at the rear of the room. The men drifted back to their conversations, voices lower and heads closer.

"Over here," called Large.

Piers turned to see the pair seated behind a pillar, invisible from the door.

He sat down. "Do you have the stuff?"

Little screwed up his face and hissed Piers quiet. "What you trying to do? Make us look like criminals?"

Large nodded. "Need to order first."

The swing doors crashed and an obese man in a not-recently-washed T-shirt walked out. He pounded straight to their table, pointed at Piers, and looked at Large. "You know?"

Large nodded. "A friend."

The obese man slapped Piers on the back. "That good."

Piers coughed as he tried to regain his breath.

The man grunted. "This no charity. You eat?"

Piers nodded and looked vainly for the menu.

The man slapped Piers on the back. "I bring food. You eat. You pay, yes?"

Piers nodded. "Of course."

"Good." The man addressed the restaurant. "It is not always that customers pay so easy." With that he stamped back through the double doors and Piers heard pots and pans clanking.

"Let me guess. Terry?"

"No. Yakof Something-or-other. He's Russian. Everyone calls him Terry, but Terry was the previous owner. He just hasn't got around to changing the sign over the door."

Little raised his eyebrows. "He's had a busy eighteen years."

"Charming guy."

Large shrugged. "Family came here before the wall came down. He refuses to learn the language, but he cooks a good breakfast."

"Do you have the car?"

Large nodded toward Little. "His car. Parked out back. Blue Citroën. Old, beat-up. I filled it with gas, in case you have to run far."

"Your car?" Piers said.

Little grunted. "And don't you forget it. I want it back without a scratch."

"I'll do my best."

"You better, Romeo. It's paid for and I'm not buying another one."

Large grunted a laugh. "Paid for."

Piers ignored the comment. "What about the other stuff?"

Large leaned forward. "Scuba gear's in the back. On loan from a friend. Don't know what you have in mind, but the tank's full."

The swing doors crashed and Yakof Something-or-other thumped down a plate and mug of tea in front of Piers. "You English, yes?"

Piers nodded.

The man gestured to the plate. "I make English breakfast. You eat."

With that, the man started working his way around the other tables, arguing with his customers and demanding payment for meals. How much the meals cost and how many bills were paid seemed to be something of a sport between the man and his patrons.

Piers ate bacon, eggs, sausages, and toast, all washed down with hot, sweet tea. It was comforting after the stress of the previous twenty-four hours. The grease settled his stomach.

"You do have a plan, don't you?" Large said.

"Get Brunwald to hand over Sidney before he gets the money."

Large frowned. "You'll both be expendable once he has the diamonds."

"I know. I'm going to be on a bridge. When he spots me, I expect he'll have his men block off the bridge. Once he's let Sidney go—"

"You're going to jump in the Seine," said Large.

"It's the only way."

"The Seine stinks," Little said.

Piers shrugged. "Nothing much I can do about that."

"The smell isn't the only thing," Large said. "The currents can be wicked."

"I'm going to float downstream. Pont Saint-Michel has a good ladder out of the water."

"Wait a minute," Little said. "You're going to be dressed in scuba gear and hoping that Brunwald doesn't notice? You're nuts."

Piers flapped his coat. "I'll cover it with this."

"And the flippers?"

Piers shrugged.

"You've got guts, kid." Large said.

"Let's just hope we don't have to wash them off the sidewalk," muttered Little.

Large glowered at him before turning back to Piers "What can we do?"

Piers gave a flat smile. "Call the police."

"What?!" said Little

"That's all?" said Large.

Piers raised his eyebrows. "Well ..."

CHAPTER TWENTY-NINE

Brunwald stared at the map while Kuznik stood at attention beside him. Petit Quai was just as its name suggested. If Piers wanted to meet there, he clearly intended to pick up the girl by boat. It was an exposed position, lots of on lookers. It didn't make it any more difficult to take the snit out, but the getaway would be more complex. He briefly considered a boat, but discounted it as he ran his fingers over the many bridges between the banks and the island Notre Dame was built on.

He tapped his finger on the map. "Here and here. Either side of the river. You'll have a good view of the handover point."

"Want me to put one in him to start?"

Brunwald smiled. "You read my mind. Nothing life-threatening until after the handover. Just make sure he knows we mean business."

"No problem."

"Once we have the diamonds, take him out."

"And the girl?"

"Her too. We don't want anyone left knowing we were here."

Kuznik gave a mirthless smile. "Trust me, it'll be my pleasure after listening to her all night."

Brunwald straightened up. "And when we have the diamonds?"

"Straight to the airfield."

"And the men?"

"They take the first plane. We take the second."

Brunwald raised his eyebrows expectantly.

Kuznik tapped his phone. "Twenty pounds of C4. Already in the hold of their aircraft. One call is all it takes. All we have to do is decide when to get rid of them."

Brunwald smiled and nodded. "You're a good man. This time tomorrow you and I will be rich Argentineans. Just make sure things go by the book."

CHAPTER THIRTY

At four-thirty, Piers parked the blue Citroën on Petit Quai. He reversed it into the narrow space, ready for a quick getaway, and took a large duffel from the trunk. He rapped on the windows and heard a rat-a-tat reply. Satisfied, he locked the car, placed the keys under a rock beside the driver's side door, and walked along the embankment road to Pont au Double.

He looked over the bridge. The narrow ledge looked even smaller as he contemplated jumping onto it with the heavy bag. He waited until a man with a dog left the bridge, then rolled over the wall. He gripped hard as he lowered his feet to the ledge, but it was still a six-foot drop. He shuffled the bag tighter onto his shoulder, held his breath, and let go.

His heart made one single, colossal beat, and his hands scraped the centuries-old stone before his feet smacked on the ledge. He grabbed at the support, and shoved his face against the stone, forcing his center of gravity inward to stop him from toppling into the water. The bag rocked on his back until he stretched his shoulders and dampened its motion.

He shuffled underneath the arch of the bridge where the ledge widened. Holding onto an iron pipe that stuck out from the wall, he lowered the duffel to the ground and slipped off his coat. With frequent curses, he managed to get the oxygen tank onto his back. He tucked the mouthpiece over his shoulder and into his shirt, out of sight but within easy reach. His coat barely covered the tank, but as he pulled it around he convinced himself that it would look like a badly-fitting jacket. He shuffled out of his shoes with ease, but lost one of the flippers in the water as he tried to put them on. Satisfied he was ready, he huddled down on the ledge and waited.

As dawn broke, the chatter of pedestrians joined the rumble of cars and lorries. He checked his phone and used the GPS coordinates to create a list of commands for the cranes. At eight o'clock, he saw Kuznik on the left bank, studying the bridge with binoculars. Piers buried his face between his knees. He knew his coat looked like crap and he probably did, too. With luck, the man would assume he was a tramp sleeping off a night's drinking. He didn't dare check for several minutes, and when he did glance back in the man's direction, he'd gone.

At five minutes to nine, a man walked down onto Petit Quai. He checked over the blue Citroën and tried the doors before making a phone call. Thirty seconds later, Brunwald's black Mercedes swept onto Petit Quai.

Piers heart raced. A wave of heat swept over him. His shirt stuck to his skin. He wiped his hands on his coat. Show time. All he had to do was follow his plan. He could feel his heart thumping in his chest. If this went wrong, Sidney would pay with her life. The air seemed to leave his body and leave his legs weak.

He took a deep breath and checked his phone one last time. A button labeled *Collect Payloads* glowed. He pressed it. The button flashed *Collecting 2 Payloads ... Stand By*, and from the corner of his eye he glimpsed movement high above.

His heart thumped and he took deep breaths, oxygenating his body and trying to calm his nerves. If he could get Sidney away from Brunwald and his men, then things would be all right. But it was a big if.

He took one last deep breath and stood up. A man on the

opposite bank turned toward him. A moment later the man on Petit Quai turned in his direction, too. Piers swallowed. Obviously, they had radios.

Piers dialed Brunwald. He answered on the first ring. "Don't do anything stupid, my friend. I still have your girl."

"Don't you do anything stupid either." Piers took the bag of diamonds from his inside pocket and held it at arm's length, out over the Seine. "Tell your goons to back off. Shoot me and the diamonds disappear forever."

Piers saw the man on Petit Quai cover his mouth and talk into a microphone. The man on the opposite bank held his hands up, then laid them on the embankment wall.

"Good," Piers said. "Now let her go."

"And why would I do that?"

"Because you have a man on either side of this bridge. Let her go and they can walk over here and take the diamonds, easy as that."

Piers waited thirty seconds and was about to speak again, when the rear door of the Mercedes opened. Sidney got out along with a man holding her by the arm.

"Tell her to take the car. The key's under a rock by the door." Piers said.

Piers heard Brunwald's curt orders drift over the water. The man marched Sidney to the car and let her go. She picked up the key and unlocked the door.

Piers hit the second button on his phone. The screen flashed *Delivering First Payload ... Stand By*. He forced himself not to look over to the giant cranes, but in his peripheral vision he caught something large and yellow, moving fast.

Sidney started the car with a lot of grinding noises from the starter motor. The man on Petit Quai pointed a gun into the car.

Piers swallowed. "Don't do anything stupid or I drop them."

"You wouldn't make it off that bridge alive," Brunwald said.

"And you wouldn't have the diamonds." Piers shook the bag at arm's length over the water.

There was a long silence, then the man lowered his gun. Sidney revved the car. The engine screamed and screamed. Piers eyes fixated on the Citroën. Why wasn't it moving? It'd been fine when he drove it. The engine revs dropped. "Just get out and walk," he whispered. "Just go, go." He wiped his forehead. The engine revs started again, this time the car shot forward, up the slope, and screeched to a halt at the embankment road. The man on the quay ran after her, pulling out his gun. Piers willed her on as he saw more yellow filling the sky. To his horror, the car raced backward. The man barely moved before the Citroën hit him. He tumbled over the trunk, rolled off, and down the slope. Then with a squealing of tires and a blaring of horns, Sidney lurched out into the traffic on the embankment road.

Yes! Piers bounced on his toes. Yes, yes! She'd made it. She was free from Brunwald and his goons. They might try to go after her, but he was prepared for that. He wanted to punch the air, but instead he pushed the third button on his phone, and the words *Delivering Second Payload ... Stand By* flashed in red.

He heard scrabbling noises from the top of the bridge.

Pain erupted in his leg. He collapsed to his knees, grunting. A storm of stone chips exploded around him.

He dropped his phone to grab his leg. There was blood on his pants and his thigh burned like hell. He bit down on his cheek. From the corner of his eye, he saw a yellow blur moving fast. Above him, boots dangled over the bridge.

He had to go. His leg howled in protest, but he shuffled to the water's edge.

There was yelling from Petit Quai. He glimpsed the crane holding the giant yellow dumpster twenty feet above Brunwald's Mercedes. The crane executed the last of his instructions, and released its payload. There was a yellow blur and the dumpster smashed into the engine compartment of Brunwald's Mercedes. The car twisted around under the weight. One of the front wheels sheared off and bounced into the Seine.

In front of him, a very black suit followed the boots, and

Kuznik dropped onto the ledge in front of Piers. The man's massive shoulders filled the narrow walkway. Piers shoved the bag of diamonds into his coat, and rolled into the Seine as Kuznik leapt forward, arms outstretched.

Piers felt the ice-cold water grip him like a metal band around his lungs. The burning pain in his leg was blotted out by the paralyzing cold. He snatched for the mouthpiece to his oxygen tank. His knees scraped against the stone bridge. He kicked with his legs, but couldn't move. Pain seared through his wound and he felt himself being lifted out of the water. He grabbed at the slippery rocks under the waterline, but in a moment he was crashing onto the narrow ledge.

Kuznik swung his boot into Piers' stomach. He felt as if a spear had been driven right through him. He doubled up, choking and gasping for breath. Bright lights danced in his vision and he squeezed his stomach to numb the pain.

He felt himself being lifted up by the lapels of his coat. He dodged left in time to blunt a blow to the face. He grabbed Kuznik's arm, but the man wrenched it back, throwing Piers to the ground. Kuznik pulled a knife and Piers scrabbled backward, deeper under the bridge. His coat caught under his hands, and he fought to stop falling onto his back. Kuznik reversed the knife in his hands and stepped forward. Piers heard the water lapping under the bridge. He was right beside it, but if he jumped, Kuznik would surely come after him. If he was going to escape the man, he had to stop him first.

Piers wrenched off his coat and whipped it around across the front of the Kuznik. The man stepped forward, slashing the coat into jagged halves with one sweep of his knife. Piers slid one arm out of the oxygen bottle's harness and flipped the bottle around his front. Kuznik lunged forward. Piers brought his knee up, lifting the bottle into the man's face. The impact felt like part slap, part crunch, but the man's long arms stretched around it. Piers felt a light flick that built to a fire raging across his chest.

Kuznik grunted, rammed the bottle back at Piers, and

slashed again. Piers dodged the blade by inches. His chest hurt like hell, but he swung the bottle from his other shoulder, freeing himself from the harness. Kuznik smashed his fists down on the bottle, ripping it from Piers' hands, and drove it, top-first, into the centuries-old stone of the bridge. There was a tearing of metal and a brief hiss, followed by a screaming roar. Kuznik didn't even move. Jet propelled by the gas pressure, the bottle smashed into his groin, doubling him over in an instant. He roared and lashed out. Piers grabbed the bottle's harness, sweeping it behind him, over his head, and down onto the giant's back. Kuznik grunted hard and dropped to his knees. He slashed at Piers' ankles. Piers leapt backward and swung the bottle again, aiming for the man's side. Kuznik brought his arm up to protect himself, but the momentum was too much. The bottle hammered into his forearm with a sickening crack. Kuznik roared and sank to the floor, his forearm unnaturally bent. Piers threw the bottle down on the man's groin. He stuffed the diamonds in his waist band, and leapt from the ledge.

The water's cold was numbing. The pain in his leg and chest grew into a fire that threatened to overwhelm him. He gasped and kicked with his good leg. His face dipped under the water. He thrashed with his hands, pulling himself just far enough out of the water to snatch a breath.

The current pulled him along, away from Kuznik and his knife. But, as he looked up, he realized his was heading out of the protection of the bridge. In a moment, he'd be visible above the water.

And Brunwald's men wouldn't let him drift away alive.

CHAPTER THIRTY-ONE

Sidney twisted the key in the ignition. The engine churned and churned before it caught. She held the key in the start position and the motor squealed in protest, jolting her into releasing the key.

She put her foot on the accelerator and the engine screamed. She kept her foot down, but the car still didn't move. The man outside held his gun on her and stepped backward. She gave him an unsure grin.

"Put in in gear, for Christ's sake," said a voice behind her.

She whipped around to see Little's face looking up at her from underneath the rear seat. "Wh— wh— what are you doing here?"

"Dying, if you don't put it in gear!"

She grabbed the transmission lever and rocked it back and forth.

"Put your foot on the brake."

She stamped on the brake and the lever bumped backward. A small display said, "Drive," so she took her foot off the brake and stamped on the accelerator.

The car lurched forward, wheels spinning. She jerked the steering wheel as the car leapt for the end of the road. The tires squealed as she struggled to take the corner and ride up the slope to the main road. Above her she glimpsed a large flash of yellow and behind her she heard a terrific crash. She turned and saw a giant, yellow dumpster crushing the front of Brunwald's Mercedes.

Little pointed forward. "Look, look, look!"

In front of her, traffic raced by on the main road.

Little pulled himself up between the front seats. "Slow down. You'll kill us."

She stamped on the brake. The Citroën nose-dived and juddered to a stop, launching Little face-first into the center console. He yelped and wrenched himself back, blood running from his nose. "What are you doing?"

"Driving! What the bloody hell does it look like?"

In the distance, police sirens sounded. With a crack, the Citroën's rear window exploded and she saw a man with a gun running up the ramp to the main road. She grabbed the gear lever, wrestled it into reverse, and stamped on the accelerator.

"Non, non, non!" screamed Little.

Sidney twisted the steering wheel and the car weaved toward the man. She saw the look on his face change to horror. He jumped, but the rear of the Citroën hit him and he crashed, face-first, onto the trunk. She stamped on the brakes. He tumbled off and rolled back down the slope to Petit Quai.

Little thumped her shoulder. "Go, go, vite vite, go!"

Sidney didn't move. She stared at the man rolling down the road. Little reached over the seats, shoved the gear lever into drive and twisted her shoulders forward. It took a moment for her to realize he was pressing on her knee, forcing it down on the accelerator. The engine roared and the car shot forward.

Pedestrians leapt aside, and traffic on the embankment road loomed again. Sidney covered her face with her hands, and felt Little shoving past her. She peered between her fingers and saw Little twisting the steering wheel away from a red car right in front of them. She stopped pressing on the accelerator and grabbed the wheel. "Let me!"

"About bloody time," Little said.

The Citroën leaned drunkenly and its tires squealed.

Little screamed "paintwork," but the side of a minivan directly in front of her held her full attention. A deep crash of heavy objects was followed by the long screech of ripping metal. She braced herself against the steering wheel, but Little flew forward, over the front seats, landing head-first in the passenger footwell.

The engine's roar died and the car bounced diagonally away from the minivan and into the oncoming traffic. Sidney screamed and twisted the wheel, attempting to perform a U-turn in the middle of the traffic while tires screeched and horns blared all around them.

Little righted himself in the passenger seat. "What the hell are you doing? This is my car!"

"Will you shut up! I'm driving."

"Driving?!"

Police sirens closed in on them. Cars weaved around Sidney's slow progress across the width of the road.

Little pushed on the steering wheel to turn faster. "Come on, come on."

"Get off! I'm doing fine," Sidney said.

"Fine? You've wrecked my car, and if you don't go faster we're going to be arrested."

"For what? This is your car."

"Are you on something? You're forgetting the bullet holes, the cars you've run into and the dumpster your boyfriend dropped on Brunwald and his apes back there. Oh, and you ran someone over for good measure."

She bumped over the curb and floored the accelerator. "You think they're going to come after us?"

"They're police, for god's sake, that's what they do—mind, mind, mind."

She looked in the direction Little was staring and saw another yellow dumpster flying through the air. "Wow."

"We have to be in front of it before it blocks the intersection. Go, go, go," he said as he pushed on the steering wheel.

"Get off!"

"Faster!"

"It's coming toward us."

"Faaasterrrr!"

Sidney pushed the accelerator down hard. The engine note changed, the gearbox dropped down, the car leaned back on its suspension, and they lunged forward, racing across the intersection. Sidney kept watch on the giant yellow dumpster and Little tried to steer them around the car in front. They clipped its rear corner, and the Citroën bounced, while the car in front veered into rapidly-braking oncoming traffic.

Behind them, Sidney caught a glimpse of yellow, dust, and debris. She felt the force of the dumpster smashing down in the middle of the intersection. It bounced once, a solid, crushing force that dug into the tarmac. Cars screeched to a halt all around it, blocking the intersection in all directions. "That could have killed us!"

"Tell that to your boyfriend."

"He's not my—where is Piers?"

"In the Seine, if he's lucky. Take the next left, Pont Saint-Michael."

Sidney kept a vice-like grip on the steering wheel. The turning was close—so close that she turned the wheel sharply. The tires squealed. So did Little. The car leaned over so far she thought it would topple, and she raced across oncoming traffic, thumped the curb, and mounted an empty patch of sidewalk.

"Stop!" Little said. "Stoooppp!"

She trod hard on the brake and the car slewed sideways to a halt, rocking back and forth on its suspension.

Little panted. "Sh- Sh- Sh-"

"What?"

"Sacre bleu! You nearly killed us! This isn't Starksy and Hutch."

"What do you expect? I can't drive. No one said I would have to drive. I didn't ask to drive. I've never driven anything before. I was expecting someone to be there to pick me up. You know, like a proper handover?"

Little slapped his hand against his forehead. "Can't drive? Now you tell me, after you've wrecked my pride a joy?"

"Like I said, no one asked me. If you'd asked me, I would have—"

"You weren't exactly easy to get hold of, you know?"

A car they had cut off drove past, its horn blaring and the driver shaking a fist at them. Sidney made a face back at the man.

Little stretched. "Besides, I risked my life by staying squashed up under that seat for the past several hours, just so I could help you get free." He gestured to his car. "And this is the thanks I get?"

Sidney gave him brief apologetic smile. "Sorry."

Little's glower softened slightly.

"Thanks." She gave him a big smile and wrapped her arms around him. He patted her shoulders before sliding his hands around her.

"Okay," she said.

"Yeah." He patted her shoulders one more time. "Come on, we need to find lover boy."

They got out of the car. Back along the embankment, she could see lines of stationary cars, honking their displeasure at the congestion. Two giant cranes loomed over the quay, their cables drifting down to the yellow dumpsters.

Sidney laughed. "Piers did that?"

Little raised his eyebrows. "Oh, yeah. Laugh a minute. Damn near killed us."

"But he didn't."

Little huffed and walked toward the middle of the bridge.

Blue flashing lights surrounded Petit Quai. Handcuffed men were being forced into the back of an armored police van. On the bridge, police were attending to a man on the ledge where Piers had stood. She strained to see.

Little produced a small pair of binoculars. "It's not him. One of Brunwald's. The big guy. Looks in a bad way."

Sidney took the binoculars and scanned the scene. "Kuznik. Couldn't have happened to a nicer person."

"You know him?"

"A bastard," she said. "Where's Piers?"

Little pointed at the Seine. "Down there somewhere."

Sidney screwed up her face. "You're serious?"

Little rolled his eyes. "I told you. He's in the Seine."

"In?"

Little leaned over the wall at the edge of the bridge. "In."

Sidney stared at the murky water. "Why's he in there?"

"Because Brunwald would have killed him if he'd been any closer."

"Is he going to be okay?"

Little looked back down into the water. "Only if he gets here in the next couple of minutes."

CHAPTER THIRTY-TWO

Piers drifted, carried by the Seine's flow. The edge of the bridge was no more than ten feet away. Another five seconds and he'd be exposed to Brunwald's men, a proverbial sitting duck, bobbing on the water.

He took deep, rapid breaths and dived down, swimming hard for the bottom. He scooped water with his hands, fighting his buoyancy. The cut on his chest burned, and his injured leg begged him to stop.

He sensed his surroundings brighten and knew he'd emerged from the shelter of the bridge. He opened his eyes for a second. The water stung, but, to his relief, all he saw was the Seine's dirty green color. If he couldn't see Brunwald's men on the bridge, they couldn't see him either.

He kicked with his good leg and renewed his struggle to keep underwater. His desire to breathe added to the pain in his chest. His arms ached and his strokes slowed. The pain in his injured leg made it useless, and he thrashed his good leg to keep himself down.

His strokes faltered. His arms trembled as if he was about to lose control. His body screamed for air and rest, but he gave one last effort, down, forward, and away from the bridge.

He curled his head onto his chest. It took every ounce of effort to stop his nose breathing in the Seine. His lungs begged him to open his mouth. His throat closed up. He had to breathe. He had to surface.

He headed upward, flailing his arms and kicking with his good leg. He thrust his head up and back, desperate. The air hit his face. His mouth burst open, spluttering and coughing. His lungs pumped his chest, sucking oxygen in a frenzy. He choked and rubbed his eyes as he whipped around to look for Brunwald's men. He breathed a sigh of relief when he saw Pont au Double was farther than he'd expected.

He forced a big draft of air into his lungs, ready to dive again, and then realized blue lights were flashing on the bridge. Large had done his job, the police would handle Brunwald and his men. He let out his breath and treaded water with his good leg, letting the current carry him. His lungs burned and his ribs felt as if they'd been stretched two sizes. His biceps and shoulders felt heavy and weak.

He'd escaped Brunwald's grasp, but had Sidney made it? She had driven away in the Citroën, and Little should have been able to direct her to the second bridge. But had they made it before the second dumpster came down?

Piers saw police on the ledge where he had fought Kuznik. They were strapping the giant to a stretcher. Piers breathed a sigh of relief. A second slower and he'd be the one being loaded onto a stretcher, probably for a short trip to the morgue.

The river carried him on. Pont Saint-Michel was only a minute away. The bridge was lined with people watching the activity around Notre Dame. He had intended to use the oxygen to keep submerged and draw less attention, but being seen was a fair exchange for making it out of Kuznik's grasp alive.

He kicked for the bridge's central support, but the arch of the bridge swept darkness over him before he reached it. The water sped up as it squeezed through the narrow part of the bridge. He dug in with cupped hands and fought the flow. The ladder's iron rungs were his only plan of escape. What had seemed easy from solid ground looked far less certain in the water.

The proverbial light at the end of the tunnel approached fast. The swirling water slowed as it began to open out. Even the overcast daylight was almost blinding as he emerged from the tunnel. He swam hard, but the water swept him away from the rungs and safety. Head down, he scooped water in his hands until he felt the rough burn of a rope flick past his wrist. He grabbed tight, and looked up to see Large's frame filling the bottom rung, the rope around his arm. Large grinned. "Need a hand?"

Piers wrapped the rope around his wrist and held on as Large dragged him to the iron ladder. He took the rungs one at a time, not daring to look up. His breath came in deep gasps. He felt the skin on his arms prickle. Would she be there? Had she made it away before Brunwald's men could give chase? Had the police stopped her? What would she say?

And would what he say?

His world had been brighter from the moment she'd jumped into the taxi. She was stunning, for sure, but she was everything he wasn't, and everything he wished he could be. She was infuriating, yet could bestow joy with a word, a smile, or the lift of an eyebrow. She could be innocent and wise at the same time. She was cool, fashionable, and fearlessly independent. He sighed, and his imagination slowed its roller coaster ride. Yes, she was independent. She was cool and fashionable and worldly, and ... and there went the stake through his heart.

He was none of those things.

He wished he were. He wished he had made more of an effort. He wished he could throw off his stupid self. Shed his fears, throw out his inhibitions. Change the day, as Bernard had said. But it was too late now. He'd done his best to save her, and now there was no reason for her to associate with him anymore. He spat out the taste of the Seine, and before he realized it, he was at the top of the ladder.

Hands grabbed at him. Little slid his arm under Piers' and pulled, but Large did all the work. Piers grunted against the pain in his leg and chest, staggered over the wall, and collapsed to his knees on the sidewalk. Pedestrians detoured around them, staring. He lifted his head and rotated his shoulders to ease the pain in his chest.

And saw her.

Her eyes were wide and her hair stuck out at angles that would have impressed a punk rocker, but her thousand-watt smile had found one more watt. A tear rolled down her cheek. Her lower lip trembled. She brushed her jumbled hair back over one ear. "Damn you," she mumbled, "Damn you, damn you, damn you, damn you."

She dropped to her knees and threw her arms around his shoulders. "I thought they'd gotten you, or that you'd drowned, or that ... You took so long, I thought they'd killed you. I thought you, you, you ... I thought ... I thought I wouldn't see you again."

He squeezed her tight and buried his face in the curve of her neck. She cried, sniffed, and thumped his back. The pain in his chest screamed, but he paid it no attention. He felt like he would melt in the warmth of her embrace.

Her tears slowed and she pulled her head back to look at him. She sniffed and laughed. "Bloody dumpsters." She wiped her nose on the back of her hand and stood up. "Bloody dumpsters."

Her eyebrows hunched together and her pupils narrowed. She swept her hand around fast, slapping him on the cheek. "Are you mad? Do you know what you did? You could have bloody killed us! Killed me! Crushed me with a bloody great dumpster on my head! What a stupid, idiotic, thick-headed ..." She bit her lip and sniffed. "... Brilliant, wonderful, fabulous ..."

She cupped her hands around his face and wiped his lips with her thumbs. "Damn you." She leaned down and kissed him, long and hard, full on the lips. She sunk to her knees and wrapped her arms around his neck. "Damn you, James Bond."

He slid his hands around her back, crossing them over and hugging her with all that remained of his might. He heard clapping, cheering, and catcalls from passersby. He didn't care. As she helped him to his feet, a smiled stretched his mouth wide and wasn't about to quit.

His shirt flapped open and blood ran down his front. She traced a finger along the slash across his chest. He put his hand on hers. "It'll be okay."

She nodded doubtfully.

Large hustled the group across the road to a crowd watching armed police officers swarm around Notre Dame. Brunwald was freed from the battered Mercedes. He pushed and shoved the officers. They pushed back. He swung a wild, looping right hook at one man, who caught Brunwald's arm, twisted it behind his back and threw him onto the ground. Several officers piled onto his arms and legs as he thrashed in vain. A few moments later, they had his hands and feet cuffed and threw him into an armored police vehicle, which departed with an escort of sirens and flashing lights.

Sidney hugged Piers. "Good riddance."

He hugged her back. "We'd better go."

Police sirens sounded behind them.

"Too late," Piers said.

Sidney looked the opposite way down the street. "This way."

Large placed his hands on her shoulders. With an upturned smile, he stared straight at Piers. "Only way to get this all sorted out, I'm afraid." Piers gave a glum nod. Sidney squirmed. Large tightened his grip and looked her in the eye. "No more running, now."

Sidney's gaze fell, her shoulders sagged. Piers took her hand. "It'll be all right."

She swallowed hard. "You're not the illegal immigrant who was helping a criminal."

Piers smiled softly. "The illegal immigrant that found a work of art, recovered a bag of diamonds, and caught Brunwald the Butcher." He put his arms around her waist and kissed her. "It will be all right."

They hugged until the police surrounded them.

CHAPTER THIRTY-THREE

The police officer led Sidney out of her cell in the women's wing of the Commissariat de Police du 5th arrondissement. The smell of cheap disinfectant was everywhere. They walked past the guards to the interview rooms as they had done each day. Sidney hated the interviews. She had begun by trying to explain everything, but that seemed to get her into more trouble, so she had clammed up. Let the police work things out for themselves.

As the officer unlocked the room, Sidney glimpsed Piers at the end of the corridor and shouted his name.

The officer shoved her into the room and slammed the door before she could figure out if Piers had seen her.

She shook herself free of the officer's grasp. "I want to talk to him."

The officer scowled. "I'm sure you do. The inspector's orders are that you two are to be kept separate, and I intend to follow that. To. The. Letter."

The officer gestured for Sidney to sit.

Sidney looked at the officer. "I just want to see him. Just a few minutes. Nothing long. You could be there. The inspector, even. I just ..."

The officer held up her hand and shook her head. "Two prime suspects in an ongoing investigation? It's not possible."

"But is he okay?"

The officer glowered at her for several seconds. "He's fine."

"Really? His chest? The knife wound—"

"I told you, he's fine."

"Will you tell him I'm thinking of him?"

The officer just stared at her.

Sidney leaned forward. "Has he asked about me?"

"I've told you all I can. What monsieur Chapman does or thinks, I cannot say."

"But ..."

The officer held up her hand. "Non. No more."

Sidney sank back in her seat. Had he asked about her? Surely the officer would tell her that much, wouldn't she? And what did she mean by "does or thinks"? Was she avoiding telling her something she wouldn't like to hear?

Sidney sighed. She knew what she didn't want to hear. Maybe the woman knew it, too. Had his emotions cooled with a week in a cell? Was that it? Was that what the woman was avoiding?

She bit her lip and mashed her hands together. She remembered everything about him. Banging heads in the shower. His stupid act to get past the police officer at Auguste's apartment then returning with a dog. Running away from the bank after he crashed the police car into their revolving door. Finding the painting.

She breathed out hard and straightened her back. He really had seemed different. Heck, he was probably the bravest person she'd ever met. He'd come back for her. Faced the dictator and his men. Saved her life. Even though she had been the one to put their lives in danger. She would never have guessed from their first moments, but he'd turned out to be a real, live James Bond.

But it had only been one day. A wild day, but just one. And was that it? Was she fading from his life like adrenaline?

The door creaked and the inspector walked in. He had a wad of papers in his hands and a pen tucked behind his ear.

"Bonjour, mademoiselle. You are ready to help us this morning, non?"

Sidney took a deep breath and stared at him. "Let's just get this over with."

CHAPTER THIRTY-FOUR

Piers heard footsteps in the corridor outside his cell. Every noise reverberated in the empty metal and concrete staging area. Footsteps had come and gone all week. Sometimes they'd been singing drunks, but often they'd been the inspector assigned to his case. This time there was no singing.

He rolled over gingerly on his bunk. The pain across his chest was almost gone. The cut had been long but not deep. His leg wasn't so good. The bullet had torn a chunk from his thigh. The doctors had dressed and stitched the wound. It would leave a scar, but the pain had gone.

Several times a day he'd asked to see Sidney, but every request had been denied. On one occasion, he had seen her disappearing through a door as he was led to an interview room. He'd shouted her name and she had turned, but the guards had closed the door before they could speak.

She had been right about the French police. They were efficient, but not in the slightest bit sympathetic to their situation. He understood. It was a tall tale and there was a trail of bodies to be explained.

An attorney had been assigned to each of them. Piece by piece, evidence had cleared them of the murders. Brunwald had been taken to The Hague to stand trial for crimes in Elbistonia. Kuznik had quickly followed, his men providing a ready stream of information when they discovered their escape route had been rigged to dispose of them in the air. The painting had been returned with much fanfare through the embassy, and Piers had glimpsed a moment of TV showing celebrations on the streets of the Elbistonian capital.

His attorney had refused to pass messages to Sidney, but in one interview he had told him the only charge she was still facing was illegal immigration. Piers had felt a great weight lift from his shoulders with that news. He had practically skipped back to his cell.

But that had been two days ago and he hadn't seen or heard of her since.

He wanted her released, of course, but what would she do? Stay in Paris? Or would the authorities force her to return to Elbistonia? Would he see her again? Would she want to see him? Her ardor had cooled rapidly when the police arrived on the bridge, and she had sunk into a paralyzing gloom. The police had been his idea, of course, and perhaps with a week in the cells she had come to blame him.

The footsteps stopped at the door to his cell. There was a knock, a rattle of keys, and the door swung open. The case inspector smiled at him. "Monsieur Chapman. Gather your things. You are being released."

Piers pried himself up, being careful not to scrape his leg on the edge of the bed, and followed the inspector to his office.

The inspector sat at his desk. "I have to ask you one more time, monsieur, the diamonds?"

Piers shrugged. "I took them after the fight with Kuznik, but when I got out of the water, they'd gone. They're in the Seine somewhere."

The inspector scowled. "A claim that guarantees the police will never find them."

"Huh?"

"Your story has filled the Seine with bounty hunters, monsieur."

"Oh." Piers shuffled.

The inspector took a deep breath. "Nevertheless, you are being released on the condition that you return if we have further questions. You understand this, yes?"

"Am I free to return home?"

The inspector leaned back in his chair, his eyebrows raised. "I am surprised you do not wish to stay in Paris, monsieur."

"You're kidding, right? I've had enough excitement, I just want to go home."

"I see. Very well." The inspector held out his passport. "This has been endorsed such that you cannot leave the EU ... but you may return to England."

The inspector signed Piers' release form with a flourish and handed it to him. "You are free to go, monsieur."

"What about Sidney?"

The inspector gestured to the doorway. "She is next."

She stood cuffed to a police officer and staring at the forms on the inspector's desk.

"Sidney." Piers felt his heart lift and fall in one sweeping movement. He held his arms out and did a good impression of a Cheshire cat, but Sidney's eyes didn't meet his. Her expression was cold and fixed.

He lowered his arms. "You okay?"

Seconds passed before she mumbled "Fine."

The police officer walked her to the inspector's desk.

Piers looked questioningly at the inspector, who waved his hand at him, "You are free to go, monsieur." He gestured to the door. "Si vous plait."

Piers was out of the police station before he realized. The sun was down and the streetlights were on. He lingered on the steps, but he wasn't sure for what.

He'd worried all week, churning acid, desperate to see and talk to her. There hadn't been a moment when he hadn't wondered how she was doing, and all she said was *fine*. One single word. He hadn't known what to expect. He'd prepared himself for joy or raging anger, but the fatalism of her voice left him numb.

He sighed. He felt as if his heart slowed a beat. She had been breathtaking. A blinding light in his ordinary world. A star too high for him to hold onto. He looked at his hands. He had tried. He had rescued her. It hadn't all gone to plan and the doctor had told him he'd be scared for life from his run-in with Kuznik, but he had saved her. He clenched his fists. She was safe. That was all that really mattered.

He heard her voice. "You're going home."

He jerked his head up. She was six feet away, arms folded. Staring at the ground between them.

He cleared his throat. "I, I guess."

"Right," she said, her head bobbing upward and her jaw barely moving.

His phone buzzed.

"Mother," Sidney said, flatly.

He rejected the call and hummed his agreement.

She stared at him, her lips thin and every muscle in her face frozen.

He took a deep breath. "I was—"

"You better get going then."

He closed his mouth slowly. "What are you going to do?"

"Does it matter?"

"I—"

"I heard you." She jerked her head toward the police station. "Back there."

He raised his shoulders, questioning.

"You said you wanted to go home. Had enough excitement, you said."

"I—"

"I guess I was just an accessory to the excitement. Thrilling for a minute."

"No. No. I mean, yes, you were part of the excitement ... but you weren't just that. I would have wanted to be with you, no matter what."

"Would have."

His mouth hung open. He stared at her face till she glanced at him. He spoke slowly. "Want, not would. I want to be with you. I've wanted to be with you since you jumped in that stupid taxi." He waved his hand at the police station. "Every moment we were in there, I wanted to see you. I worried about you. What was happening to you. What would happen to you."

She grunted. "And you still want to go home."

"Eventually ... One day."

She looked sideways at him. He thought he saw her lip quiver. He held out his hands. "But not today. And not tomorrow. Maybe not next week, and—"

"The week after?"

Their eyes met and he saw a sliver of a smile growing radiant. She tilted her head up, and he saw tears spilling over a thousand watts. He flung his arms around her.

"I thought you were going to bloody leave," she said. She crushed him in her embrace, pounded on his back with her fists, and forced her lips painfully on his. He felt the pounding of her heart.

He pulled back from her, and stroked her hair back over her ear. He squeezed her tight and laughed. "Would I dare?"

She punched his shoulder. He wiped away her tears with his thumbs, and they kissed, tender and gentle, long and hard, their tongues touching and exploring. He ran his hands through her hair and down her back. The feel of her curves under his palms overwhelmed him. He felt as if he couldn't breathe out. She gripped his belt and pulled him upward and tighter to her. He closed his eyes, drank in the smell of her skin, and the world ceased to exist.

Minutes passed before a shrill voice called out, "Get a room."

They ignored it.

A car horn sounded. "Really, get a room."

Their eyes wandered reluctantly in the direction of the voice.

Little and Large were leaning against the side of a bright yellow car. Large opened the rear door. "Taxi?"

"No!" Sidney laughed, taking a step back.

Piers smiled. "It'll be all right."

She stared. "Look what happened last time."

"Yeah, look," he said, smiling.

She squeezed his hand. "Yes."

He dipped down and swept her up in his arms. She squealed as she looped her arms around his neck and held on. "What are you doing?"

He grinned as he walked to the car. "Something I should have done with you when I had the chance."

Her eyebrows bunched together and she twisted in his arms. "What do you think I am, some easy—"

He held her tight, juggling to keep her from falling. "Dancing, I meant dancing."

She froze, her hand on his shoulder and her mouth open. "Oh."

He raised his eyebrows. "At Bernard's?"

"Right." She bit her lip and nodded. Her smile returned, soft and warm. "Dancing," Her eyes locked on his and her fingers played through his hair. "Mmmmm, yes," she said, "You can take me dancing."

She nipped at the lobe of his ear. Her breath tingled his spine and he curled his head toward her reflexively. His lungs felt as if they would burst, and he had to swallow before he could speak. "And then?"

She lowered her head onto his shoulder and patted his chest. "We'll see, lover boy. We'll see."

PARLE MOI!

Make me happy.
Tell me if you liked it,
Tell me if you didn't,
And tell me what you think happened to the diamonds.
I'd *love* to hear.

... aka
Please leave a review wherever you purchased this book ☺

Merci!

ABOUT THE AUTHOR

Nigel Blackwell is ashamed to say he hasn't been to Elbistonia, danced at Bernard's, or jumped in the Seine, but he has cavorted in and out of wetsuits in freezing weather, raced against the traffic down one-way streets in Paris, and eaten at Terry's All Time. He also keeps a set of bolt croppers to deal with the problems these actives can bring.

But he's not telling what happened to the diamonds.

Yet.

facebook.com/authorNigelBlackwell

twitter.com/@Nigel_Blackwell

Printed in Great Britain
by Amazon

56299982R00138